T0197234

Cracker Chronicles

"Casting a Long Shadow"

R. Wayne Tanner

*Our mission is to efficiently provide the world's finest, most comprehensive book publishing
service, enabling every author to experience success. To find out how to publish your book,
your way, and have it available worldwide, visit us online at www.trafford.com*

Trafford rev. 08/30/2010

www.trafford.com

North America & international
toll-free: 1 888 232 4444 (USA & Canada)
phone: 250 383 6864 ♦ fax: 812 355 4082

CHAPTER 1

The storm clouds of a great conflict between a lifestyle that had been practiced for generations and the invasion of a new way of life with its boundaries of barbed wire and restrictions begins to appear on the horizon. The weary cowman stands in the shadow of what once was his, hat in hand and watches in disbelief as the winds build to gale strength, a wind that will soon destroy the structure of life deeply loved by so many. The clouds churn high in the sky clearly visible to all that are willing to see. But to those unwilling and convinced this could not be happening are caught unprepared and perish in its wake. The occasional rumbles of thunder in the form of conflict and misunderstanding erupted across the once peaceful scrubs, hammocks and swamps within the boundary of this rapidly changing world. Men and families who had worked closely together for generations and who willingly cooperated in building what little they needed to survive now stand in stark opposition to each other. Men who had never spent one moment of their life worrying about anything now spend sleepless nights staring into campfires trying hard to figure out ways to face the next day without controversy. They once carried guns as protection from the predators such as bears, wolves and panthers now ride alert to the possibility of being fired upon by their neighbors and strangers who want to force themselves into their world. Those who had fought together to preserve the Confederacy now look at each other as hated as those who invaded their home causing them to flee further south again to unrestricted freedom.

Between 1823 and 1935 men braved the wilderness of Florida hacking out a living for themselves and their families. There were no established law other than the self imposed restrictions placed upon one another in order to maintain good manners and some sort of harmony. If anyone; regardless of race or color violated the country philosophy of "live and let live" were dealt with by the strong arm of common sense justice. For example, if a man harmed or neglected his wife or children the surrounding neighbors would step in and hold him accountable or else. If someone was caught stealing for any other reason than to feed his family he was dealt with harshly and at times hung for taking from another's mouth. Thus the establishment of the clan, even though the writer does not agree with what it has become or the cruelty committed, he does agree with how at its first organization it protected the innocent no matter their color. No foolishness was tolerated nor mercy extended to a willful and repeating violator. Personnel vices as long as not misused were overlooked but those who without care of another and persisted were swiftly dealt with. Rustlers and thieves where considered as bad as murders. Mischief was over looked until it brought harm to the innocent.

It all began to change for the peace loving and secluded Florida Cracker when rich men from up north began to take notice of the advantages of living in and developing this so called tropical paradise. Areas of barren land useless for farming or grazing cattle which lie along the west and south east coast had great appeal. The railroad cut its path through open scrub land and across wide span of nothingness delivering innovation and people by the car loads. Dredging machines were brought in. The continual rumbling of the large engines filled the land and drew the curious stare of settler and Indian alike from their seclusion and hiding. The land mass grew right before the unbelieving eye of the native Floridian. Men and women dressed in strange garments began to buy up land and not even knowing what they were buying. The timber company's sight unseen purchased hundreds of thousands of acres hacking down tall virgin pines and draining the massive swamps for the great bald cypress trees. Turpentine camps sprung up all across the scrub sending billowing black smoke into the sky and filling the surrounding area with a putrefying stench only leaving behind hundreds of unmarked graves, a scared scrub and defaced pine trees in its wake.

When the timber companies would buy the land, regardless of how long a family had worked to improve the land they were told to leave carrying only that they could tote. In all reality they were forced to leave and many thought this to be unfair. This became one of the reasons why the violence. Finally when Florida was granted statehood the timber companies were made to deed a squatting family forty acres and to pay the new land owners for the timber. This helped some, but for some it was already too late. Anger grew and resentment toward those who invaded their once peaceful life, now seen as enemies, enemies that could not be dealt with because of greed on the invaders side and the limited resources of the Florida Cracker. While researching for this book I recall hearing a story of a family who had improved almost two hundred acres of harsh back woods. They had a successful farm including a fifty acre orange grove were forced to pack up and leave because the father just could not grasp the idea of someone owning the land God had blessed them with. Much less could anyone convince him and many tried that he could have easily purchased the land, but he never would accept it until it was too late. Sixty years of struggle faded in the distance as armed guards escorted them off their land in just two days. Within two months the old man had died and many of his children believe it was because of a broken heart. There is a happy ending, they moved south and purchased thousands of acres and vowed to never be force to move again.

Those who had taken part or had family members who had taken part in the Seminole Indian Wars now know what it must have felt like for the Indian when others forced their will and desires upon them.

This is but a glimpse at that struggle and how it not only impacted men and their families but a way of life that can still be seen in many parts of Florida if one is willing to take time and look. Cowboys still saddle their horses and drive to an old set of cow pens and spend many an hour atop their favorite horse gathering, working and selling a new calf crop. They string miles of barbed wire and drive thousands of staples in fence rows built by their grandfathers and great grandfathers. To many, thou, it is lost and only a fading dream. Deep in the soul of Florida lies a great heritage called the ***True Florida Cracker.*** Not the urbanized rednecks that can afford a pair of Wrangler jeans, a shiny belt buckle, a fancy felt hat and black pointed toed cowboy boots but the true country boy and girl. Those who know the reason why you carry a pocket knife, how to keep it sharp and not cut yourself. Those who can appreciate a good pot of collard greens without the sweet cornbread you buy in a box. Those who are not afraid of taking a firm hold on a catfish as it flops around and taking out the hook without getting stuck. To those who had actually stepped into a fresh pile of cow crap and knows what it smells like and in a way appreciates the experience. To those who were taught to say "yes mam" and "no sir" and remember what respect is. To those who say to themselves that they were born in the wrong time.

There is one era of time in Florida history that changed the face of the cattle business and has affected the Florida of yesteryear. Out of all the happening that shaped this great state only one stands out as decisive as the Texas Tick Fever. In the years between 1899 and 1925 a silent intruder invaded the peaceful hammocks and scrubs of Florida. Up until this point in time and the development of the Florida cattle industry few predators had caused as much trouble as this tiny pest. Indians caused their share of danger and the rustler before, during and after the War Between the States and up until the mid 1950's caused the Cracker Cowmen their share of trouble as well. But none pushed the Cracker Cowman further and harder and cost him more than the Texas Tick. I do not claim to be an expert on the subject but all that I have read and the conversation I have had with those who experienced just moments of time within this period all agree, this changed Florida.

Florida had all but exhausted the wild cattle population which was the main source of replacement cattle for the Cracker Cowmen. After selling last year's calves and estimating the losses due to natural causes the Cracker Cowmen would just go into the open ranges of Florida, find cows without a mark; marking them as their own without a second thought. Someone though came up with the bright idea of bring cattle from the states out west. They did and as a result these cattle soon learned to thrive in the lush grasses of north, central and south Florida marshes and open scrubs also brought with them a tribulation that would challenge some cracker cowmen to their last breath. Along with the new supply of cattle came the Texas Tick Fever and screw worm epidemic that changed the face of Florida Cracker Cowmen forever.

What happened to the smaller cowmen who could not afford the costly requirements of the government simply faded away into loving a life style lost to them forever with a pain deep that will last for many generations, while the wealthier land owning cattleman bought the herds of the smaller cattlemen forcing them to make another adjustment in their over burdened life. Uprooting families, who had depended upon the illusive cattle that once roamed free for the taking around the homestead that had been a part of their family for close to one hundred long hard years! Most of the children had to abandon the life they loved to seek employment away from home, while others refused and stubbornly held to a way of life that was in all of their blood. The war was almost a welcomed distraction that again stole from families that had already given a lot more than others. Many who are two and three generations removed from that life style still hold the dream of one day having their own herd of cattle, working them and smelling the singed hair of a freshly branded cow. But, it is only a dream that every Monday they awake from and head back to life.

Chapter 2

Wiley and Mollie Tanner watched daily as their little boy who they proudly named Malachi Pistol Tanner grew. You need to understand that this was not easy in the time they lived. A time one had to work every day all day long just to have enough to eat. Place on top of that the frail physical condition of this little boy, growing at all was a miracle. He struggled at first with eating. They tried everything but as soon as he would swallow his food he would violently vomit it back up. Because of this he was considered a runt, for that reason he never grew very big. There were nights his breathing was so labored seeing another day was uncertain. His mother would hold him setting up giving him only temporary relief. Aunt Rose the local mid-wife and several of the older women of the settlement in South Georgia would come at night to relieve the exhausted mother spending the entire night bathing sweat from his brow, rocking him and praying for a miracle.

He would wheeze so loudly at night his mother would find it difficult to sleep for watching him. He was sick a lot the first three years of his life running high fevers that Aunt Rose would find challenging to break. Mollie prayed daily that God would spare his life and allow her the chance to raise her baby boy. The pain of watching the torture his child had to endure drove his father to drinking. When he drank he would become violent. Aunt Rose grew tired of his ugliness and told a few of the men in the settlement which quickly brought a harsh reprisal and a warning to straighten his self up or they would do it for him. The thought of being revisited caused Wiley to stay away from the booze for a time. He then filled his time with farming but found little peace in the weariness he daily experienced.

Something happened while Aunt Rose was caring for the baby during the spring of his third year. Early one morning as the two women ate, sipping on a steaming hot cup of coffee and talking casually they heard the baby cooing. This was strange to them and startled them because the only noise he had ever made up to this point was a loud wheezing and continual raspy cough. Mollie reluctantly rose from the table, her heart beat so loud within her chest. Standing for a moment she steadied herself, slips into the room and to her surprise and delight there lying on the pallet on the floor was her little pale baby boy smiling and cooing and spitting and slobbering. Mollie fell to her knees dropping her face into her hands and began to sob tears of joy. The thought of her sickly child having the strength to smile was so overwhelming. She called for Aunt Rose, her shrill outburst frightened her. The old women shuffled along reluctantly but as fast as she could and saw the miracle. The word miracle was the only word she could think to describe what happened that morning. She lifts the child into her arms holding her weathered leathery hand on his back, nothing. Just yesterday she could feel crackling now there is nothing, nothing, but calm deep unlabored breaths of the weak little boy and she smiles. A single tear rolls down the wrinkled weathered cheek as she closes her eyes and breaths a prayer of thanksgiving. She extends her arms out before her and examines the boy and the first thing she notices were the pink cheek and a sparkle in his eye. Mollie will always believe God touched him that morning and healed him, because God Himself must have a great purpose for this young child's life.

Malachi always ate like a horse, almost as if he was starving and this did not change. No matter how much he ate he still looked as if he would always be stunted. He would never grow to the size of his father. He never overcome or grew out of looking in poor health but he never lacked in strengthened and was as active as any other boy his age. If it crossed his mind he would do it. Mischievous, was a word that best described this little boy who had a lot to make up for. His size and courage proved to be a source of ridicule from the other children. This frustrated Malachi and his mother would always tell him they were only jealous, of which he just could not understand. He wore tattered clothes that never fit well, never had enough in his lunch pale and had a father who was the laughing stock of the settlement. To him jealousy must be a powerful thing if it can cause a person to over look what a man appears to be on the outside and sees something else, blinding them to reality. Malachi vowed to never practice this meanness called jealousy.

He would sit for hours trying to figure a way to become equal with all the other boys. While at the store near their home a stranger noticed how the other boys picked on Malachi and stepped in he chased off the aggressors. He could see the frustration in the young boy's eyes along, taking note his size. With a calm voice that caused Malachi to immediately calm then relax the man invited him to sit and talk. While he sat on the edge of the porch they spoke for a few minutes when the stranger reached into his satchel and handed Malachi a long shiny knife. Malachi turned the knife over and over in his hands, admiring its shape and length. The old man smiled, than his expression changed. Placed his wrinkled hand atop Malachi's and the knife assuring him this makes all men equal and must cautiously used, making Malachi swear to be careful. He awkwardly smiles unsure as to why this stranger would give him such a gift and promised. Before he could properly thank him he simply disappeared down the street. His first thought was how he was going to sneak the big knife into his home. His mother abhorred violence and tried to teach him from a young age vengeance belongs to God. He wishes he could get his mother to understand, he needed someone or something a little closer than God.

When he was not doing his chores he practiced throwing the large knife. He became proficient in its use and his aim became more accurate as his confidence grew. He was able to throw the knife both over and under handed. As quick as it cleared his belt it was in flight in the direction of whatever he aimed to hit. With pinpoint accuracy it would strike its mark every time. He could hit toads at fifteen feet. His mother caught him one day and excoriated him for having the knife and tried to take it from him. Malachi was able to escape and ran into the woods, fearing the consequences when he returned but to him it will be worth it. He spent the next few nights wandering the woods around their home while Mollie cried and prayed next to the fire. Late the first night Malachi used the knife and cut palmetto fans laying them over a thick cover of fox grape vines. He crawled under just as a little drizzle began to fall. He shivers and begins to feel himself getting sick. He coughs and for the first time sees blood in his hand and becomes frightened. He tries to take a deep breath but all he could do was cough. His heart beats rapidly pounding out of his chest. The spell lasted for a few minutes, exhausted he fell into a deep sleep. Wiley had searched every inch of every bend of the small creek and asked if anyone had seen his boy. Unaware of his continual coughing his father was able to locate him. As he picked him up the knife fell into the leaves hidden from view. Just about midnight the front door of the modest cabin swung open, a gust of cool wind blew into the small room making the fire in the stove shift and yield to its influence. There standing in the doorway Wiley held tightly in his arms their unconscious dirty boy of eleven years. Blood stained the corners of his mouth. His mother jumps from the chair next to the fire causing it to fall against the table sliding down with a crash grabbed him from his father's arms smothering him with her rather robust frame. His father was relieved yet determined in his belief the boy needed punishing even if he was repentant. No child should put his parents through what Malachi had caused. It took several days to recover from this bought of sickness. His mother waited patiently bathing his brow, feeding him steaming hot potato soup while his father stood by growing angry with every passing minute. The longer he stood there the madder he became due to the trouble he had caused. Two weeks past and things seemed to revert back to normal until one morning his father burst into the cabin holding a peach limb. He grabbed Malachi from the table dragging him out into the yard. His mother had never been an aggressive woman but this morning something possessed her and she lit into Malachi's father causing him to drop Malachi to the ground knocking the wind from him. Wiley did all he could to fight off his wife until he finally gave up on his intention of punishing Malachi. From that day on Wiley was careful not to riyal his wife or bring up his belief that Malachi needed punishing. The reason for all the trouble faded from his parent's memory, but not from Malachi's. Never forgetting the big knife he slipped from the house early one morning. Retracted his steps and uncovered the large knife now stained by spots of rust. Relieved and proudly he grabs it and aimlessly walks back toward the house. He opened the front door and surprisingly there sitting at the table was his father. Before he could conceal the knife, he stood and walked toward the boy. Malachi stopped and stood defiant as his father reached for the knife pulling it from his waistband. As he withdraws it the knife slices through his thin breaches and right into his thigh. As the knife sliced through cutting him the boy never flinched or cried out. His father was dazed by his son's stubbornness, at the fact he did not flinch as the blade sliced through his leg. A chill ran down his spine mixed strangely with a deep since of pride in that he had succeed in hardening Malachi for the life he was going to have to face. His mother watched from the shadows and wept because she knew that a man needs compassion and that was one lesson Malachi was having trouble learning.

She lowers her head, turns and walks away. Without expression Malachi looked down, touches the wound with one of his fingers, slowly lifts it to his nose and takes a deep breath. After she tended his wound she put him to bed retreating to her room, she shut the door and prayed until she fell asleep. She agonized over the heartless and senseless actions of her husband and child. She hated her husband but knew she could not live like this and dismissed her feeling and prayed that her Malachi would not turn bad.

His father waited until the next morning and walked down to the creek tossing the knife into the deepest hole he knew. Unaware, the boy stood in the shadows marking the spot where the ripples finally disappeared, a spot to which he would return soon and retrieve his knife.

Life soon returned again to as normal as they became accustomed to. The cut on Malachi's thigh healed slowly, leaving just a small scar. He was able to return to school where once again the cruelty intensified by the older boys. Malachi was helpless in defending himself until one day he picked up a stick that was well balanced in his hand and he met his aggressors, challenging them. They readily accepted his challenge to which Malachi firmly learned he was no match with just a stick, even though he was able to hit his mark on several occasions. His effort only left him bleeding and his clothes almost ripped from his body. The humiliation of the beating and the fact that he had to walk through town almost naked caused a callousness to form in his heart. He was satisfied with the whipping he received because he was able to draw some blood from those who hurt him. He staggered home, washed himself at the well, threw his tattered shirt behind the wood pile knowing he would have to face the question to where was his shirt but for the moment it was to hurtful of a reminder and vowed this would never happen to him again. There was no school the next day. Even though Malachi was extremely sore, with one eyes almost swollen shut and a deep purple ringed with yellow he finished his chores without saying a word or one utter of complaint. Just after lunch he sought permission from his father to go to the creek to fish and for a swim. Permission was granted and off Malachi ran in the direction of the creek. It was slightly more humid then the days before. Malachi had to stop and cough several times but quickly recovered and continued forward.

Malachi stood at the spot his father had stood several weeks before discarding the knife. Taking off his cloths he stood on the bank of the deep creek feeling the hot sun wash over his body. It was at these times unrestricted by anything that he felt the freest and the sickness that sat in his chest could not faze him. Just before he dove into the water he looked down at the scare on his thigh and smiled, then disappeared under the surface of the water. It took several tries before he located the knife stuck in the white sandy bottom. Just before he was about to lose his breath, he grabs the knife, placing his feet firmly on the bottom and pushes his now exhausted body like a rocket to the surface. As he broke the surface he took a deep breath. Using his free hand he wiped the water that flooded from his shaggy hair from his eyes as he swims to the bank. Gently he lays his prize next to his clothes, turns and casually swims back and forth across the creek. In his mind he is satisfied that everything will be ok. Slipping effortlessly from the water he reclines back on the grassy bank enjoying the sun as it warms his body. Closing his eyes shielding them from the bright sun he falls asleep and immediately dreams.

Something wakes him with a start. Without thought he grabs the knife, whorls and stands in a defensive stance. There standing not five feet from him was an elderly man holding a fishing pole and stringer of catfish. Both were shocked at the encounter but Malachi's surprise turned to embarrassment when he realized he stood before the stranger completely naked. Scrambling for his clothes he drops the knife pulling on the tattered overalls. In the rush both legs find the same hole causing Malachi to lose his balance and topples to one side hitting the ground with a thud. Hurrying back to his feet he turns again toward the man now red faced. The old man speaks with a voice of instruction. "Don't ever drop your defenses, no matter the circumstances." With lightening speed he drops his fish reaching down picking up the knife. Malachi was scared but defiant enough not to turn and run. The old man admires the knife turning it over and over in his hands examining the knife than commenting on its size and sharpness. The boy reaches for the knife as the old man pulls it away from him asking sharply. "What you doing with such a big knife?" He waits for Malachi's answer as the boy fumbles for the right words. Relaxing he shares with him as to how he got the knife and how the man who gave it to him said it would help him to be equal with anyone who would challenge him. With the nod of his head the old man agreed and reminded him as to why he told him to never drop his defenses in any situation even if he was standing naked. He went on to say. "Without your knife you are as anyone. This can only help you if it stays in your hand. Do you understand what I am telling you?" Malachi shook his head in agreeing with the man and they sat and talked for several hours. Malachi had never felt as comfortable around anyone as he did that afternoon. For the first time in his entire life he believed in himself and felt as if he had something worth saying. All of a sudden it dawned on him that it was getting late. Well aware he would most likely get in trouble he politely dismissed himself and ran as fast as he could back toward the house but before he got too far he turned to wave good-bye but there was no one there. He stopped in his tracks because the old man just suddenly disappeared.

Everything seemed a little brighter that afternoon. The orange clay staining his bare feet seemed not as hot and annoying. To Malachi life was as good as it could be. Dismissing any thought of the trouble he might met at the hands of his father he raced home.

As he expected his father was waiting for him as he rounded the corner of the garden plot. Luckily he had stashed the knife in some brush just off the trail. His father questioned him as to what he had been doing and why he was gone so long. Malachi told him of the old man and how he just lost track of time. Before he could say another word his father slapped him to the ground. He hit the ground with a thud. The pain was great and he laid there motionless. Mollie watched the whole thing from her vantage point on the porch. She brushes past her husband almost knocking him to the ground and not fearing his reaction. Like a guardian angel she bends down, gathers the boy in her arms straightens up and stares at his bleeding lip. She then turns and glares defiantly right into her husband's hate filled eyes. Undoubtedly he clearly understood what she meant by her audacious stare then turns without saying another word. Her heart beats faster as all the emotions and adrenaline she was experiencing stirs inside her. As she walks toward the house she notices for the first time in a long time the frail state of her child. Gently she lays him down on the ground next to the well knowing this was no time for the tears she feels rushing to the surface. She wipes her eyes and withdrew a fresh cool bucket of water from the deep open well. She removed her apron, dipping it into the bucket and washes his face when finally he was aroused. He stares at her as a single tear rolls down his cheek. The look in his eyes was easily recognized by Mollie because every time she looks into the mirror she sees that same expression. Malachi begins to cough. He struggled to catch his breath and Mollie sees for the first time the blood in his small hands. This scares Mollie. Leaning down she franticly questions him about how long this had been happening. He turns away not wanting to look at her and lie to her face. She forces his head back around insisting he look at her and tell her the truth. He told her she did not have to worry that it had only happened a few times before. He wipes his hand on his dirty overalls gets up and heads toward the barn to do his chores.

CHAPTER 3

The moon was now high in the sky and shining brightly, illuminating the entire clearing. Shadows darted from one side of the yard to the other. The screech owl screams out sending chills up and down Malachi's back. The whippoorwill called out only to be answered off in the distance by another. Malachi became restless on his seemingly endless watch for the morning to dawn. The screen door squeaks as he swings open the door stepping out into the clearing in front of the house. He stares up into the sky becoming dizzy as he watches the flickering of the stars. Small clouds race across the sky like ghost. Turning in all directions he located certain stars, audibly calling out the directions they were in. This information will serve him well in his life to come. If a person can determine the direction they were headed then that person will never truly be lost no matter where they were. Off in the distance he could hear the constant hoot of the owl and shivered. He never liked to hear the owl because it was too mournful. Again shivers run over his body as he rubs his warm hands up and down his boney arms. He wishes the morning would come soon. Streaks of light rise shooting high into the eastern sky. The darkness is soon replaced by the moving shadows cast by the rising sun. The last hoot fades as it is replaced by the song bird's song. He strains his eyes looking for the source of the echo of the caws of the crows as they pass over head to places unknown.

The heavy dew fell during the long night and the cold wind caught everyone by surprise. It produced a deep frost covering the ground in a white blanket. As usual Malachi was called from his warm bed and sent to the wood pile to fetch and replace the wood used during the night. The old stove was the only source of heat in the drafty house. Many a night

Malachi would lie in bed and stare out through the gaps in the wall. The spiders would appear and disappear in the cracks and killing them had become one of Malachi's favorite pastimes.

Taking the gloves his mother had sown for him out of a coarse salt sack. Before putting them on he rubbed his hands together in front of the stove trying hard to thaw his boney fingers. Even though he had been inside the since early morning it was still close to freezing in his room just off the cooking area.

He sits on his favorite old wooden stool given him by his grandfather. He was a gifted carpenter and had built many of the pieces of furniture in their home. The only skill he would like to have inherited from his grandfather but Malachi could not even drive a nail straight. When he was just a little boy the stool helped him to sit at the table his grandfather had also built. Effortlessly he pulls on socks his mother had woven out of some cotton she had gleaned from behind the Negro hired to labor at harvest time. Malachi could never remember receiving any other Christmas gift other than clothes. He reaches for his hand-me-down brogan boots. Patches cover the holes. He was thankful for the boots because just last year as he would drive the milk cows to pasture he would have to run from one fresh dropped cow pile to another just to thaw out his frozen feet. His cold feet ached as he slipped his feet into them even though they were too big for his feet. The thick socks helped them not to slip on his heel saving him from blisters. When he first got the boots from his uncle they caused huge blisters on his left heel that almost crippled him. His mother used what little salt she could spare and packed the blister so it would heal to a callus.

Just as he finished tying the last knot his father opened the door allowing the cold to invade the warmth of the cooking area and barked another order at Malachi. He stood quickly not wanting to agitate his father and answered with a respectful reply. "Yes sir". He had learned early in life and knew better than to speak any other way than respectful and reverent. He did not want to irritate his short tempered father. Without hesitation he went about completing the task his father had ordered. It was a foregone conclusion he would ultimately get in trouble for not filling the wood box which was his first chore for his mother but knew better then to delay the completion of what his father had assigned. The cold air made it hard for Malachi to breath. He hurried toward the open well, looking in the direction of the old trail leading out into the large pines and scrub prairie. He had thought of running but dismissed the notion as quickly as it entered his mind. He was often accused of day-dreaming too much and the terror he experienced regarding the short temper of his father kept him from doing what he really wanted to do. As he rushed between the well where he would hoist heavy buckets of water from deep in the ground using a long sweep to the cow pens holding several head of cattle his father had just traded two slaves for. He could hear the crunch of the frost crackling under foot and could not wait until spring came when the days were longer and warmer, leading to summer. With each step his arms ached and his hands burning from the cold splashing water. He had taken off the gloves because he knew he would have to wear them all day long and did not want them to be wet. He looks down while holding his hands out and took note of how red they were and the feeling of numbness. Out of the corner of his eye he noticed his mother at the wood pile, lifting arm loads of cut wood, righting herself as she nearly stumbled. Malachi drops his hands and runs to where she was leaning next to the barn. Taking the stove wood from her arms she smiles at him and complements him on how hard he worked. She touches his cheek and tells him she was extremely proud of him and how much she loved him. It took two more trips to the wood pile before the box next to the stove was filled.

The kitchen bustled with the activities of everyday life, what would be considered noise to some was a symphony of beautiful sound to young Malachi. His mother was beyond belief she could prepare a meal out of just about anything. Malachi loved watching her magic. Breakfast consisted of white salt bacon, grits milled from the community grit's mill and hoe-cake covered with the caramel colored sugarcane syrup. Cane syrup has a taste of its own, almost salty and looks almost a burnt brown. To some it is bitter but if you had never tasted maple syrup you would think you were eating the best there was. Malachi ate the portion dished to him without saying a word. His father would place on the children's plate what he wanted them to have. It seemed his father would only give Malachi small portions and often he would leave the table hungry. With every bite he thought to himself, knowing not to say it out loud, of the time when he will be able to leave this place, provide for himself and never come back. The only thing keeping him from running away now was his love and devotion for his mother and the fear she would probably be blamed for his leaving and punished. The thought of the abuse his mother would have to suffer was motivation for not fleeing.

Mollie noticed the distant look in young Malachi's eyes. Deep down inside she knows when the time is right he will leave out on some adventure;

which will take him far from home. She fears that when he finally leaves she will never again see him. Thinking of when he was just ten years old.

After finally completing his daily chores and sure there were no surprise assignments he would head for the woods surrounding the clap-board shanty given to his father as a part of his personal servitude and hell they all lived daily. (His father started out owning several hundred acres of good bottom farm land but lost it because of his inability to stop drinking the rot gut shine. One day he accidently shot a man. The man who claimed to be his so called best friend paid the fine to get him out of jail. The final payment was the land he owned and for him to share-crop to payback the debt. Willingly and knowing the extent of the agreement he entered into this arrangement with the man who now owns the land. The arrangement was forty percent of his crops for twenty years. It has now been over thirty years and with each passing year Malachi's father grows more bitter and mean. He takes his anger out by striking at anyone he feels crosses him, this includes Malachi. As soon as Malachi was old enough he entered the fields and toted water. Learning to hitch the mules and in due course began plowing. It took less than a year for Malachi to become convinced he would never live like this especially under the control of another man.)

Malachi would often return home well after dark. Mollie could hear the familiar squeak of the long sweep as he lowered it and drew water from the well. She earlier had placed the few pieces of whatever meat she had prepared for their supper out along with a cold biscuit beside the low burning oil lamp and disappeared into the shadows. Many times she would blissfully watch him hungrily eat. Other times she would just go ahead to bed and lay alongside her sleeping husband knowing that her favorite son was home and safe. Mollie hated the night because it was in these long quiet hours she thought of killing her abusive husband. In her mind she had buried a knife deep into his chest, watching as he struggles to take a breath. Then she wakes in a cold sweat her heart beating wildly in her chest whispers a prayer of repentance begging God to give her patience. Other times she could imagine taking the cast iron frying pan and as he slept she would beat him to death only to repeat the nightly ritual of asking for forgiveness. She wondered if this was normal and asked Aunt Rose about it only to be met with silence. She feared she was meant for this personal hell and resigned herself to it. Until late one night two weeks later while everyone slept the door of the cabin was crashed in and several hooded men rushed in and before Malachi's father could reach his gun leaning against the wall at the front door he was drug from the house and into the darkness. The surprise and swiftness of the incident horrified everyone and it was not until late the next day they learned of the reason. Wiley was beaten and warned one last time that his wife and children were not his to abuse. He confided in Aunt Rose who told Mollie about it and promised that if he touched her or Malachi again she would have him killed and she was serious about what she said.

Days turn into weeks, weeks into months, and months turn into years as Malachi's skill as a woodsmen and tracker were being honed. Just a few days after Malachi turned sixteen years old his responsibilities increased that involved taking more trips by himself into the closet settlement to their home called "Coffee". Malachi stood only five feet four inches tall. His spindly frame was over shadowed by the long knife he now carried openly for all to see. One day his mother called him from the small garden he planted for family use instructing him in detail on trading the precious few eggs she was able to gather and save. She wanted them delivered with care and traded for salt and two spools of thread. Malachi was proud of his mother because she had earned a reputation as one of the best seamstress in the area. She prided herself in her skill at weaving as well. She worked just as hard keeping her family's ragged clothes looking clean. She often would tell Malachi, (a name she had called him every since he was a little boy) that all she wanted in life was for him to grow up and be respected and when she died to be called a Proverbs 31 women. Malachi never knew what she meant until he took down her old worn Bible and read Proverbs 31 and as far as he was concerned she had always been, a Proverbs 31 women. The thread he was to get was for a surprise of a new shirt she had planned for Malachi and his brother.

Malachi experienced something he had never known before when he started up the trail toward Coffee, freedom. Old dreams flooded his mind now that he was able to escape the confines of the farm. He had never been afraid of work or did he ever try to find an excuse to avoid it, but his dreams were always somewhere else. The trip down the old deep rutted dirt road seemed shorter than usual. He noticed the birds sang a little louder than he ever remembered. To him life was good.

As he approached the store he noticed a regiment of shabby dressed men mounted on the skinniest horses he had ever seen. Their intentions were to water and rest their weary horses because they had been chasing a nomadic enemy who knew better every back trail and water hole between here and the Suwannee River to the south. The soldier standing nearest the door of the store was grubby looking, a boy not much older than himself.

In his dead hallow eyes even Malachi recognized absolute heartlessness. His eyes reminded him of the rabbet dog his father had killed last year. The dirty clad lad nudged the man standing next to him with his elbow in order to gain his attention before rushing toward Malachi without warning or provocation. The stranger for no reason grabbed Malachi's basket of eggs, forcibly taking his charge. He had never struggled with anyone who had such strength. Stunned and surprised although aware he must do something fast or lose the eggs his mother expected to be traded. Does this stranger not now these eggs are the only means of securing salt and thread? With one swift motion Malachi pulled the razor sharp knife from his belt. His knife is kept razor sharp so the blade easily sliced through the front of the tattered shirt then dragging across the now confused boy's chest. Blood oozed down the front of his chest. The suddenness of this reprisal astonished those standing near and enraging his attacker. The soldier cried out with a blood curdling scream, evil shot from his eyes and he went into a murderous rage. Uncontrollable he lunged at Malachi only to feel the second then third slice of the big knife and each one was deeper than the one before. He was in shock, stunned that his advance was met with such a harsh reaction. One of the other soldiers grabbed Malachi quickly disarming him than with a solid hit to the head knocked him to the ground. Dazed his eye swelled shut in a matter of seconds and the burning pain he experienced was unlike any he had ever known. As quickly as he hit the ground he was up standing in a defensive stance ready for the next attack. His stubbornness was met by deafening laughter because no one could believe such a small boy dared stand against full grown men. There was one impressed by his grit, the captain stood watching the ruckus, he did not intend for it to escalate beyond this point. The young man now bleeding stood flabbergasted and in disbelief. Reaching down and touching the gaping wound and again became infuriated when the ridicule came from his comrades. Panic set in for Malachi as he stumbled forward because there was not much time to react when the enraged boy drew his pistol aiming it right at his head. The captain stepped forward and shouted the order to the release of the boy before things went any further. Malachi scurried back to his feet staggering back all the while looking down at the now broken eggs there lying on the front porch. Now Malachi's eyes flashed with anger as he stepped toward his assailant wanting him to know he no longer feared him but hated him and wanted him to hurt as bad as his eye and pride felt. The captain stepped forward into the path of Malachi and chuckled while saying. "You better be glad we took that big knife from him because I believe he would cut you in half if he could get at you. Now put away that gun fore I take it from you and use it on you. Do you understand me, soldier?" His comment was met again with thunderous laughter that did nothing to ease the situation. It only put the two boys on a track that would eventually lead to a confrontation.

The captain could see the disappointment in the boy's eyes; which swiftly changed to controlled rage. The stern voice of the captain drew Malachi's attention away from the broken eggs but the main reason was to keep him from doing what he was thinking. He asked what the eggs were worth. Malachi answered harshly and began to tell how his mother trusted him enough to send him to trade for salt and thread. As Malachi answered the captain, one of the men dismounted and walked over to where the knife had fallen, picked it up wiping the blood stain from the knife on his pants leg and handed it back. Malachi stepped back not understanding the gesture then reached out taking the knife he replaced it in his belt. Turning in his direction the Captain ordered Malachi to follow him into the store, without hesitation he followed. Once inside he told him to order what he needed and it would be purchased for him. As they turned to leave the Captain asked what his name was but before the boy could speak the man behind the counter said. "Malachi Tanner, you getten in trouble again? Boy, you are getten as bad as yer pa." Disregarding the comment the store owner made the boy introduced his self as Malachi Tanner. The captain said. "Well! Hell boy. Tanner is the last name of the fella we been looken fer. I hear'd you're a good tracker. Ya need a job?" Malachi just stared without saying a word. He was taken aback by the question. Stuttering he told him he did not think his father would allow him to leave the farm right now. "It's the middle of worken the cotton and my pa needs me." The captain explained to the boy he had heard of his reputation as a tracker. After meeting a man named Ben Tanner, the newly appointed sheriff of the Coffee County. "He talked about you guiding him on a turkey hunt and how impressed he was with your knowledge of the woods. I knew you are the man for the job." He scratched his head and said confused. "But, one thing I didn't figure on was ya being so young." With a shrug of his shoulders he went on to say. "What the hell, it don't matter, I need ya. That is if ya can do the job."

With each word the captain spoke Malachi was drawn in. He had dreamed of this chance all his life. He followed him to the front steps of the old store. They sat down and talked for a good long time about nothing. The captain grew irritated by Malachi fiddling with the package wrapped in brown paper when finally he reached out placing his hand on Malachi's and said. "Hell boy, stop that yer maken me nervous. Ya don't have to go if'en ya don't want to. If go'ens gonna make ya that uneasy, hell's bell's boy." All of a sudden Malachi jumps to his feet, apologetically excusing himself trying to explain to the captain as he walked away how he needed to go or he would get a good beating. This was the first time the captain saw anything that resembled fear. Before he could question the boy he was gone. But just before he left he told the captain where he lived and asked if he could give him the rest of the day and he would gladly go with him.

It was close to five mile to his home and Malachi hurried home as fast as he could. He does not remember his feet ever touching the ground. There seemed to be a spring to his step, a freedom he had never known. He ran past the garden then right into the clearing sweat poured from his forehead and his hair was sopping wet. His face was crimson red whether by the sun or the run it does not matter. His eye was still swollen shut. His mother noticed the smile wider than the St. Marks River to the south.

She was alarmed by the sight of his eye yet it had been years since she last time she saw a smile on his face. He ran to his mother and stood just staring at her then placed the items he had traded for in her hands and kissed her. She was surprised by what he had done. She questioned him again about his eye but he was not interested in doing anything other than finishing his chores.

Her heart skipped a beat because she sensed something happened while he was away to change her boy into a man. The smile, the black eye, the kiss, she looked after him confused and filled with questions. She recalled the times Malachi had confided in him about his dream of one day leaving the farm and exploring Florida. He spoke often of possibly moving there to so he could one day become a rich cowman. Deep inside she knew her adventurous son would soon leave and she would probably never see him again, something she was not ready for. He stopped, turned and ran back almost knocking her down. She laughed placing her hands on his shoulders forcing him to take a step backward. She looked into his eyes and asked. "Yer leaven ain't ya?" He smiled that wide smile and shook his head yes. After a few moments his expression changed and assured her he would be fine and will one day return. With that he turned and continued with his assigned chores. She lifted her hands to her face hoping in some way to conceal the flood of tears rolling down her leathery cheek. The one thing; which helped her to deal with her heart ache was his excitement because it was so contagious she almost wished she could go. Before the sun set that day she too had captured his enthusiasm and she busied herself with the preparation of his departure but her heart still was breaking. She readied herself because she knew she would have to stand between her husband and Malachi's plan. She could never understand why his father despised him so, why he tried everything in his power to discourage and tear down the boy. Malachi was a hard worker and there is not one selfish bone in his body because with what little money he made, he willingly sharing so the family would not starve. Both were surprised by Malachi's father's reaction; which actually at first hurt Malachi but gave him greater resolve to leave and never look back even though he would truly miss his mother. Malachi's father picked out the best of his horses, in order for his son to be well mounted in a new country. As he handed the reins to Malachi he mumbled under his breath a remark only he could not hear. Malachi was glad he could not hear him because he did not want his disparaging remarks to haunt him. This generosity confused the boy but willingly accepted the gift as deserving. His mother went about packing what food they could spare so he would not want for anything until he was able to receive his first pay.

He stood holding the reins of a gray mare facing his mother, the wind causing her faded yellow dress to wave to and fro. She peered from underneath her sun baked bonnet offering the slightest of smiles as he reaches out and wipes away the tears as they glisten and rolling down her cheek. She leans her head in the direction of his touch and closes her eyes. The heartache she felt when she lost her first child is the pain and loneliness she feels again. Reaching out she grabs his hand with hers and weeps out loud. He draws her close and whispers so only she could hear as he admonishes her not to cry but to remember him in her prayers. For the first time all day she finds some peace when she heard him mention prayer. She was so afraid her teaching on prayer had fallen on deaf ears. He thanks her for being such a good mother and she swells with pride. As always he is able to interject humor into the situation by telling her now he might be able gain a little weight, to which both of them smiled. The statement was meant to lighten the moment but it only irritated an already grave situation regarding his father. She tries to smile again when Malachi takes her in his arms assuring her he would be ok and back as soon as possible. Once again she draws strength from her favorite son, straightens herself, shaking her head in response to his request. She had become so dependent on her oldest son realizing he was the only sure source of steady income for the family at times. She knows her faith will be challenged and is she strong enough by herself.

He leaped onto the horses back with one movement. She turns in that direction to which he brings her under control. His mother places one hand on his leg while handing him a small Bible with the other. Malachi sees his mother take a deep breath then tells him she believes in what she taught him, warning him to never forget the One she taught him of. Drawing from her faith she holds back the tears she wanted desperately to shed. At that moment she feels the hand of her youngest son slip into hers, it as if Malachi's little brother assumed the position of encourager and strength. His gesture and timeliness gave her the strength she needed to raise a weary hand and wave to Malachi as he rounds the corn crib that soon will be needing filled with the corn still standing wilted by the extreme heat they had been experiencing. She turns and looks into the dark brown eyes of her youngest son and smiles. He tugs on her then wraps his tiny arms around her as best he could. She is amazed by these little gentlemen she has had the privilege to raise are so much different than their father to which she was extremely grateful. She dismisses herself finding refuge in the only place she can be alone and that was the outhouse behind the now lonely house. The place she once looked at with promise now robs her of every drop of drive. Immediately a torrent of tears broke loss and she cries not for her lose but for her son she will probably never see again. She will have to figure a way to fill the empty hole in her heart as she whispers a prayer to her best friend; which is the LORD she trusted and needs now more than ever.

For as long as Malachi could remember he had heard what his father had often called exaggerated stories of the new unexplored territory to the south. His nights were filled with dreams of adventure in this new country. He figured if anything the warmer climate would be good for him. Story after story of Florida being filled with wild Indians and the adventure of seeing a new strange people filled his imagination. Deer and turkey filling the low hammocks around his home, a place he learned to love the outdoors but the stories told of the wild game being too numerous for him to visualize in his mind. Wild cattle of every shape and color roamed the country side, free for the taking. He had met a man who had traveled south a poor man only to return years later having more money than ever he could use. More land just waiting for someone to claim it. He was told the ground is so fertile it takes little effort to produce enough food for a family to survive. He gasps at the thought and longed to go and see.

Once while delivering eggs to the store in Coffee he was given a juicy orange from Florida. The round orange fruit was shared with his mother. She smiled while telling him she had never eaten anything with such flavor. They laughed as the juices ran down their chin enjoying every last drop. The man who gave it to him told of how they grew wild and sweet everywhere you looked. Malachi had never tasted anything like the sweet juicy orange and had often imagined sitting and eating all he wanted. They spoke of bananas, avocados and guavas of which he could only imagine what they tasted or even looked like. His mouth watered just thinking about it. Certain times of the year the creek bottoms and swamps were filled with large white blooms as big as dinner plates filling the air with a sweet pungent aroma. Yellow flowering vines cover trees sending forth its powerful smell to a point of intoxication. Honey bees could be heard for several hundred yards as they make their honey in the holes in large trees.

He would stare at himself in his mothers faded mirror and try to visualize himself in new clothes because the possibility of becoming wealthy is a prospect for any person willing to work long and hard for it. Malachi was never afraid of work and looked forward to one day having his own place, a place where he may one day bring his mother and she can just sit back a do nothing but eat oranges.

The only thing standing in his way was his hot tempered father and savage Indians who had been continually harassed for many years, first by the Spaniards, then British Dragoons and now the vile and heartless white men who do not understand the innate need the Indians had to survive. Knowing his father it would probably be easier to face a wild Indian then to have to deal with his father much longer.

(For generations Indian Chiefs and the small family bands herded cattle and depended upon them grazing freely as the main stay of their people's existence. A nomadic people believed the land could not be owned by anyone because it was a gift from the Great Spirit. The Indian could not comprehend nor were there words in their language describing the greed demonstrated by the careless whites they viewed as invaders and savages. It was a word they would soon come to use defining every white man regardless of his position in life.)

Malachi wanted to co-exist with the Indians and would learn later in his life how that was possible.

The first night away from home was spent alone camping just off the main trail leading to Coffee. Being warned by his father just before he faded into the corn field to be on his guard at all times and trust the gut. This lesson would be the first of many he would learn while on his own for the first time. That night he kept his fire concealed well out of sight of any passer-by. He did not want to invite trouble. He learned this could be accomplished by digging a hole next to a thicket shielding the reflection of the fire. This also allowed the light produced by the fire to be quickly doused. There were mean men in the world Malachi lived in who would just as soon kill you for little to nothing than to tolerate any foolishness. The local Indians, even though Malachi had never seen any around learned for their survival had become treacherous and they do not care what you are doing you where to be hated. In their mind a small white boy was just as capable of harming them as a full grown white man. Just passing through their territory was provocation enough for them to wipe out an entire family and running off their stock.

The sun began to set behind the tall pines to the west of the sandy trial. As soon as it was completely dark Malachi's heart begun to race as he felt uncalled-for anxiety. This was the first time he had experienced this feeling his entire life. Deep down inside he wished he had not left home. He was now feeling the excitement of the day catching up with him and knew it would be easier if he fell asleep as soon as he could. He was hungry but was also use to the feeling and learned at an early age to sleep through the pain. He gathered what dried pine branches and pine cones close to his camp. With his foot he clears away the pine straw strewn over the ground piling them off to one side to use for his bed. Using the small spade his father given him he rooted out a hole. He began to sweat as he hacked through the dense roots. Finally the hole was complete. A good fire was burning so he secured his horse with a hobble. He knew by experience the need to carefully hobble the horse because she horse was prone to leave him afoot. That is one aggravation he could not afford so he rechecked both knots. As he turned and headed back to the fire a wide smile crossed his face as he remembers his father having to walk about six miles home due to the horse leaving him stranded. Malachi could hear him cussing a mile away as he tripped through the darkness finally staggering up the steps. Malachi dare not laugh to where his father could hear but that next morning he gave the horse an extra dried corn cob as a reward. Malachi knew in his heart this was wrong but it made passing the time of his father's aggravation a little easier.

Content with her restrains she avariciously ate what little corn he placed in the wallet hanging over her neck. Satisfied she had gotten ever last piece of corn she turned her attention to the grass growing just a few feet away from his camp. All night long he could hear her chomping of the grass giving him some comfort. Tossing a few more pieces of dried wood on the fire he unrolled his bedroll his mother had packed, thankful she did so because the nights this time of the year could drop off cold. During the night the temperature dipped into the twenties and Malachi began to question himself again whether he had made the right decision to leaving like he did.

With the excitement of the day and the distance he had traveled sleep came easy. Malachi's first night as a man was filled with dreams of fortune.

CHAPTER 4

Malachi's first trip into the new territory of Florida began by way of the old Coffee Road. Recruited to scout and run survey lines for the Federal government. He was responsible for gathering information on the whereabouts of Indian camps and mapping any trail frequently or occasionally used by anyone who could not be identified. His favorite responsibility was to provide fresh meat for camp. His skills at tracking and killing deer and hogs had been keenly developed by spending time in the woods around his childhood home in South Georgia. His closest friend was a boy named Lehigh Simmons and they spent hours together dreaming of one day going to the land south of them and live in the wilderness miles away from anyone else. Lehigh died as a young teenager from a tooth infection. Everything was ok one minute then the next his face swelled. He suffered extreme pain. Malachi would visit with him and talk to him. You could smell the rot in his mouth. Malachi's mother explained to him the infection move throughout his body, got into his blood and that is what killed him. This was the first time any of the children had to deal with death and it would not be their last. Lehigh's mother became so distraught she hung herself. After her death she was taken down and buried outside the cemeteries fence. Folks feared suicide and believed if someone killed their self they automatically went straight to hell.

Seeing her hang there from the oak in their back yard affected Malachi more than losing his best friend. His own mother tried hard to explain it to Malachi but he just could not grasp the idea of someone killing themselves. He remembers clearly the preacher telling them all at the funeral. "If ya kill yer self, ya go to hell." Malachi could not understand why anyone would sentence themselves to hell. But in a way understood the torture she must have felt and had nothing but pity for her.

Because of his age most of the men in his assigned regiment did not trust him. Daily his commanding officer used him in spite of their questions only to prove a point. The points he made thou were painful for Malachi. Malachi had a hard time proving himself and the harder he tried the more distance grew between him and the others.

Early one morning while searching for a deer he had shot while it was on the run, Malachi happened across a well concealed and frequently used trail. It crossed through a small pond still holding water from the last rain and the water was still stirred up and in the areas were hogs had recently rooted there was sign of unshod horses. Confident this could be the very band of renegades they had been chasing, the same bunch believed to be responsible for the death of many settlers. With this information the regiment was able to set an ambush; which allowed them to kill six Indians. The information resulted as well in saving every one of his fellow troopers life cementing his place in the regiment. From that instance on he was thoroughly trusted and everyone grew dependent on the sharpness of his eyes and his skill. He no longer had time to hunt for fresh meat so while passing by a small settlement south of Madison the Captain hired a boy to do the hunting. Two weeks had past and the boy left early one morning to kill a deer they had seen but never returned. Everyone figured something had happened to him but was not allowed until the next morning to search for him. Malachi and a man by the name of Jim Cotton found him tied to a tree naked bound by deer hid. His hands tied behind him and his feet spread and staked wide apart. He was castrated and an arrow driven deep into the tree he was tied too. Malachi could never erase the expression on the boys face. It was one of pain and terror. Jim Cotton cried the whole time while they cut him free and buried him. He would never tell Malachi why he acted so strange for a boy he did not know or care to know while in camp.

It took three weeks to make their way down to Pensacola, there the men had a few days furlough. If it was closer Malachi would have preferred to go home and see his mother but there was no way he could make it there and back in such a short period of time. Malachi did slip away from the others and camped on the whitest sand he had ever seen over-looking what the Captain had called the Gulf of Mexico. One of the first things Malachi realized were the small bugs bit him feverishly even through his long sleeve shirt, aggravating him until he was finally forced to built a large fire. Using green moss he was able to produce a steady flow of smoke. This helped to drive the no-see-em's away as long as he stayed in the smoke. The smoke caused him to cough so he was forced to find refugee from the biting bugs some other way. He found the right distraction as he sat for hours watching a home-made corn cob bobber dance and bob on top of the waves washing upon the shore. He sat in awe because he had never experienced a sun set as beautiful as the one he watched that evening. The blue of the water and the sky was a sight he was sure his mother would have enjoyed. The large amber orb gave the illusion of sinking into the water. It sent its reflection off the water making the clouds appear to take on a grayish-purple tint streaked with beams of red and orange. Mesmerized by the beauty of this sunset his thoughts flashed back to his childhood home and his loving mother. Oh, how he loved his mother and it seems she is continually in his thoughts lately. Not wanting to leave the beach for many reasons but the main one was because he had finally figured out how to catch the allusive flat fish that scooted across the bottom of the clear water.

He had eaten his share of fish but had never tasted any as good as the flat fish roosted over the open coals. That night Malachi listened to the splashing of fish just off shore. Straining hard to make out what was making the noise, every once in a while the moon would reflect off of fish as they leaped from the water. The next morning schools of the jumping fish passed within feet of the shore, Malachi tried everything short of shooting into the water to see if they were as good to eat as the flat fish, but to no avail. By eating the fresh fish Malachi could feel his strength return to his weary body. On the third morning he knew he could not stay any longer so he broke camp. Reluctantly saddled his horse, dosed the fire making sure there were no smoldering coals that could blow onto the dry scrub and ignite a fire.

The palmettos along the shore were different from the ones growing on the scrubs back home. The small oak trees were so inter-laced that to pass through was near impossible. Riding back to the settlement took longer than it did a few nights before as he took his time exploring his surroundings. The willow ponds were extremely dense as they drop sharply in elevation. One minute Malachi would be riding high and dry the next slip down a wash out into waist deep water. Putting his heels to the flank of his horse causing her to lunge forward hopping one, two and on the third time finally freeing herself from the stale, duckweed covered water. As she reached the top she eyed the rattlesnake coiled, side stepped nearly dislodging Malachi from his saddle. Malachi's first reaction was to take his whip and punish the horse until he realized her sidestepping saved his life. Patting her on the neck he tried to comfort the horse while trying hard to bring her under control. His voice took on a comforting tone and she relaxed.

He had traveled several miles when his surrounding started to become familiar to him. He was able now to relax knowing the Indians had not yet started raiding this far north. At long last he rode into the clearing when his captain rode up to him a little irritated with his long absence informing him that they would be leaving in two days. Before he turned he commanded Malachi to follow him.

Malachi received his orders to ride east along the sandy ridge that emptied into a large scrub and find an open way across. It should take about one day to travel the distance and his captain expected him back by noon the next day. He hoped he would have the information he needed. Malachi wondered what he meant by that statement and asked him to clarify. He called him into his office and excoriated Malachi for questioning him in front of the other men. Telling him next time he had an inquirer to ask permission to speak privately. The captain sat in silence for a moment then speaks again knowing he felt comfortable with the young man and unthreatened. Malachi listens as he complains about the pressure he was getting from Washington regarding the trouble caused by the Indians of which he sympathized with. Regardless he had a job to do and outlined the consequences for not meeting their expectations. He dismissed Malachi shaking his hand almost pleading with him to bring back information so they could finally leave this desolate place.

Gathering what supplies he needed; which included a pound of coffee, salt, some honey, a small pot and a cast iron frying pan. These where the only things he could comfortably fit in his wallet, he needed no meat because he would kill on the trail what he needed. Malachi rode out the same trail he had entered several days before. He remembers a natural opening through the thick palmettos onto the sandy scrub filled with the blue scrub jay barking their objection to his presence. This time of year the scrub was filled with a pink flower that was real sticky. He recalls seeing a small rein caught in the flower and watches as it struggles to free its self. He tried to free it but only managed to hurry its death pulling the feathers from its side. The palmettos had longer than usual jagged edges as sharp as razors and ripped at his home spun britches like they were cheese cloth. The large stout briars would even stop his horse at times forcing him to seek another way. Large clumps of Spanish bayonet would stick deep into his legs. The pain was almost unbearable. The horse would fight against the painful spears throwing him to the ground on one occasion knocking the breath from him.

During this time of the year the sea myrtles bloomed. The stout breeze caused pollen as thick as smoke to cross the open ponds irritating Malachi's eyes but this helped him to move up wind undetected. Since coming to the more humid climate Malachi had not had as difficult time breathing.

At night he could barely get any rest due to the mosquitoes due to the deafening roar of their tiny wings. Extremely thankful for the army issued net used to protect him from the biting bugs. He had learned to use the dry cow patties as a means of repellent but feared using them because they might draw unwanted attention.

The next morning he discovered a serious of dry ponds leading due east for approximately twenty miles. While warily traversing the open ponds he stayed well hidden behind myrtles watching two separate bands of Indians using an obscured trail a good way off the main road about a mile to the east. Unaware of his presence they spoke in their native tongue. He believed them to be men, just as he because they laughed and joked with each other. For the first time in his life he question all he had ever heard about this people, wondering if they were just left alone would they kill as much.

He watched in amazement as they effortlessly moved through the thick underbrush. They rode their horses as if they were one. Convinced if this people were not his enemy they would be a people he would learn to admire. A sense of duty pressed him so his thoughts turned to leading the regiment back to this place. Malachi took a mental note of his surroundings marking the exact location by noticing the type and shape of the trees. Maybe they could surprise their enemy and rid this area of any trouble makers. He stayed in his kneeling position until he was sure they had left the area. Carefully and quietly leading his horse still further away so not give his position away, he knew by himself he could not fend off the entire bunch.

About noon the next day he emerged from the thick palmetto flat woods. His britches legs stained with blood, ripped beyond repair. The sun was high in the sky Malachi had finally experienced the extreme heat, sweat rolled down his face and the dust from the trail covering him making his clothes look even dirtier than they actually were. Riding directly to the captain's residence, he reported what he had found. The captain rose from his desk where he was seated shocked at the sight of Malachi. He gave his report and was sent to the general mercantile where Malachi was able to purchase new britches, two shirts, boots and a new gray felt hat. Standing in the full length mirror he burst with pride at his new clothes. This was the first time in his twenty years having clothes and boots that actually fit. He returned to the captain's residence and spoke again with the captain and each had a renewed hope in completing their assigned task and returning home soon. The captain called for the clerk and issued orders to prepare the troops for departure at first light. Malachi was given a piece of paper to draw the area the best he could remember. Malachi dropped his head embarrassed by the fact he could not read or write. The captain spoke vociferously to Malachi, telling him even a baby could draw lines, when in anger and embarrassment he grabbed the pencil and scratched a detailed map. The detail impressed even the local teacher who had agreed to begin teaching Malachi how to read. He took to reading and before long he had mastered the skill. He was more accomplished in it than those who had spent years in school.

Before the sun broke the horizon the next morning they were in the saddle heading east. The morning sunrise was as breathtaking as the morning before with streaks of amber outlining the cottony white clouds shooting high into the sky. The back drop of blue was brilliant. Malachi was nerves, the entire regiment and operation depended on his ability to lead them directly to where he had found the Indians the day before. He was familiar with this feeling but stayed focused not wanting to be distracted taking the straightest way there. The sun rose high in the sky driving the hovering fog to dissipate as the first of the troopers entered the open switch-grass ponds leading further east. Echoes of complaints could be heard as they passed too close to the bayonets. The horses did not like the constant poking, many protested by pitching their rider to the ground. Thunderous laughter could be heard as it echoed off the tall pines and towering palmettos bordering the pond until they captain spoke bring order back to the column. Unfortunate for them they had ridden quietly for several miles as they rounded the last clump of palmettos they came face to face with three Indians as they passed driving several stolen cows before them. Both the troopers and Indians were caught off guard and surprised. The hesitation of the troops allowed the Indians to escape before any shots could be fired. This annoyed the captain as he cussed furiously. He believed their mission was now compromised. Raising his voice Malachi rode up next to the captain calming him slightly and spoke up convincing the captain to allow he and a few others could ride now and catch up with them. He believed he would be able to stop them from informing the other. Everyone knew if the Indians ever thought anyone other than themselves knew about this place they would change their travel route and it would take longer to put an end to this irritation. He reluctantly agreed and without any hesitation Malachi led five troops in the opposite direction the Indian's had escaped. Malachi's horse was more sure footed them the bigger military horses slowing their advance until they rounded a thick myrtle bed and there in a muddy trail stood the three Indians they were searching for. This time Malachi and the soldiers were ready and through a hail of fire, two Indians lie dead in the muddy path. The other was able to wheel and run. His horse moved without much effort in and around the thick palmettos quickly disappearing. The cows they were driving moved within the area blocking the escape. Before anyone could say another word Malachi's horse lunged forward and overtook the wounded rider he was able to knock him from his horse. Before the befuddled Indian could get back to his feet Malachi sails from his horse plunging the large knife deep into his chest. The smell of the fresh blood mixed with the mud sickened him as he lay atop the dying Indian looking into his hallow eyes as he takes his last breath. Malachi began to cough violently almost losing his breath. This type of dizziness he had never experienced before. In the back ground almost muffled shouts of victory filled the air as the oldest of the troopers reached out lifting Malachi to his feet handing him a canteen. Between coughs he was able to wash the dust from his throat and the stench of mud and blood from his senses. His brand new shirt now stained with the blood of an un-named enemy. He reached down and pulled the knife from the dead man making a suction sound loud enough to quiet the men. Malachi tried not to look into the lifeless eyes still wide open but something drew his glance. Malachi jumps as someone pats him on the back. One of the older men assured Malachi killing will get easier, to which he answered. "I hope not." Then he turned to catch his horse that had run off and stopped to eat some fresh grass. The events of that day solidified Malachi Tanner's reputation and helped him to grow up.

Malachi never talked much anyhow but for the next several days he was silent and stayed to himself. Report was given and everyone was satisfied with the facts. A map was drawn by the help of Malachi through the thick brush to the main trial leading from Tallahassee to Madison. With this discovery they were able to slow the rustling of the settler livestock and curtail most of the Indian activity. It was also discovered that some of the so-called Indian activity was actually white men posing as Indians. Many believe if these cruel men would not act this way the Indian difficulty would be clear up soon, but there was still a lot of misunderstanding. One of the greatest moves the governor made was to prosecute these violators and seeking their execution. Ten men were all hung the same day and everyone was invited to watch. By this single act some Indians began to trust the white man and were willing to share the vast space between the two big waters along with the plentiful cattle roaming the open scrubs.

Under a new leader of all Florida troops; Brigadier General William Harney formed Malachi's regiment, called Rogers Regiment. This new regiment was under the leadership of Captain Robert Bullock. Not long after become a scout for this regiment it was ordered to take seven more trips into the new territory mapping new trails and locating the secluded Indians camps. The way was hard and the trails few. Some old Indian trails were located and Malachi and the others spend a better part of a year cutting and hacking through dense undergrowth so wagons of supplies could pass. It also helped to deter ambush attacks by the Indians due to the openness of the area. It was not until the fall they arrived at Fort Gatlin. This was the hub of all military activity in the region. While stationed at Fort Gatlin near a small settlement named, "Orlando" they spent two weeks at the fort. Malachi was given an assignment to scout to the east perfectly content with spending his time alone.

Right in the middle of an open scrubs west of the Econlockhatchee River he happened onto a well used alligator cave. The white sand was heaped high around the mouth of a hole in the middle of palmettos offering the only continual source of water for miles around. It was quite evident by the sign (the marks made and left by the movement of a animal) a big gator made this hole his home. He wanted to see the gator but time would not allow him the chance. As he started to ride away he watched as a sow and her shoats make their way through the knee high palmettos toward the water hole. Curious he waits until they passed, dismounted and carefully slips to where he could watch what would happen next. Reluctantly and aware of danger the sow approached the water hesitating but her thirst was too much and pushed her on. Vigilant for any sign of the monster that inhabited the cave she drank hurriedly then retreated. Each of her offspring took their turn when the natural instinct of a hog took over and the last of the shoats (a small hog that had not reached adulthood) plunged into the water splashing around. Malachi heart now beat wildly knowing something was about to happen. The hesitation of the others swiftly faded and within just a few seconds two more joined their brother. Malachi began to relax when all of a sudden the water erupted as the biggest gator he had ever seen leaped from under the unsuspecting shoats. The silence of the scrub was broken by the shrill squealing of the unfortunate one followed by the desperate grunting of the startled mother. Malachi jumped as the massive jaws clamped down on the shinny slick black form and instantaneously the muddy water turned to a bright red. Watching in disbelief as the once silent scrub still echoed with the squeal then soon silenced as the gator and the shoat vanished under the surface of the water. He shivered wondering what other surprise lies beyond the next turn. One thing for sure he will now be more aware of his surroundings, especially when it comes to crossing the dark tannic water of the creeks in this area.

The ride back to the fort was filled with new found discoveries of the possible dangers lurking around each bend and under each bush. A couple hours after the gator attack he happened to cross paths with the biggest rattlesnake he had ever seen. The pungent musky odor of the large rattlesnake sickened him and hung heavy on the warm air. The loud buzzing of his rattles sent Malachi into panic mode. His horse jumped sideways almost dislodging him from the saddle. Malachi could literally feel the horse shiver under the saddle. Patting her on the neck he spoke calmly to her hoping to calm her. Instantly he was brought back to reality because he knew a foolish man will not survive an encounter with a rattlesnake. Not wanting to waste a shot, plus he did not want to give away his position if someone other than he was on the scrub. Picking up a good stout piece of lightered (aged pine) he whacked behind the long snake. The first attempt misses. His failure was quickly met with a backward strike almost hitting his square in the chest. Luckily he was slightly faster in his response than the snake. Without hesitation he moved in front of the snake causing it to coil. The rattles sang loud. With the next blow the massive snakes head smashed and he lies dead. A valuable lesson learned to never approach a rattlesnake from behind because he can strike backward the distance of its body. In front he can only strike what he has recoiled.

He studied the only maps detailing the terrine, trails. The newest map indicated two rivers almost side by side running north and south. He noticed a well marked trail leading from a settlement to the south called Kissimmee ending at Curryville. The trail runs through Fort Christmas. Having three day left before he was expected back at Fort Gatlin he made up his mind to explore these rivers in spite of the present dangers. Following the only trail leading east, late the second afternoon away from Fort Gatlin he took into account that the landscape was changing and the large pine trees, palmettos and scrub oaks are replaced with cabbage trees, cedars, bays and magnolias.

It was not difficult to find the first river. He was amazed this river actually appeared as if it flowed north but in all reality it flows east. He was so fascinated by its beauty and tranquility. He stopped on one of the high banks of the Econlockhatchee River and spent the next several days exploring and mapping the area. While walking along the small trail paralleling the gently flowing tannic creek, his eye caught movement coming down the creek. Instantly drop to his knees. It was an man wearing brightly colored tunic and deer hid shirt that flood past his knees. From his vantage point it appears as if the man was floating just above the surface of the water. Hiding behind an old oak that had blown over sometime in the past, he could get a good look when he realized it was a Seminole Indian gliding effortlessly in a small canoe, he would later learn was a dug out. As fate would have it just as he passed where Malachi was hiding he coughed. The Indian in the canoe lifted the pole in his hand causing the canoe to hesitated a moment. He acted as if he was not sure what he had just heard then continued down the creek and disappeared around the bend. Malachi was amazed by the gracefulness of the man as he poled along effortlessly dipping and squatting to avoid the over hung branches and fallen trees across the river. He wondered his origin and if he was friendly. He wanted to call out to him but his past experience dictated that he remain hidden. The stranger disappeared as quickly as he had appeared and this made Malachi nervous. It suddenly dawned on him the stranger had seen his camp and now wondered why he did not stop and investigate the strange noise he knew he heard. He back tracked finding his horse and camp still intact. Malachi's concern was to get as much distance between himself and the stranger. Even though he admired him for his skills he knew they could never be friends. Reluctantly he left the area vowing to one day return with his family.

Chapter 5

Malachi continued to serve with this particular regiment for two full years before he could withdraw his appointment. Reluctantly his captain agreed to his discharge and promised him a job if he ever wanted it. At the age of nineteen he returned home. The entire trip home his excitement grew because he could not wait to see his mother. Malachi's heart beat steady in his chest as he made the last turn toward home. The house had begun to fall down and the dog fennels were head high. Indifferently he stepped onto the front porch only to hear the familiar squeak of the loose boards. This brought a slight smile because his mind flooded with memories of how he as a child he would sail from the ground to this very spot. It was these times he felt as if he could fly. He reached for the rope used as a latch and pulled but the door was nailed shut. He turns and calls out for his mother but no response. He walked around the house he found the back door off its hinges. He passed through to find what little furniture left covered with dust. It looks as if no one had lived here for quite a while. Fear rushed over him as he turns and walks straight toward the family burial plot where he helped to bury three of his baby brothers. The trail now covered with thick grape vines. By the time he made his way to the graves scared he would find his mother buried there. Only one new grave was there and it as his father. Finding no one he headed for the store were several years ago his adventure started. When he arrived he learned his father had died several months earlier as a result of being kicked in the head while hooking the trace chains to a rank mule. Malachi never felt sorrow for his father because deep down inside he truly hated his father. The beatings he received by his hands were too many to count. Something Malachi had tried hard to forget.

He learned his mother was forced to leave their home. She was unable to fulfill her husband's original obligation. All of the kids were now gone and she was forgotten. The neighbors living around her knew she was a good woman and were outraged by the action of the land owner but knew it was no use in objecting. Malachi learned she was forced to leave with only that she could carry. He wanted to take revenge for this heartless actions but his experience in the military taught him that execution is only as good as the plan. Right then his concern was the well being of his aging mother who now lived in a small dilapidated one room shed behind his oldest half-brother's home. Malachi was out raged by the way his mother was being treated by everyone and the way his mother looked truly frightened him. He questioned his brother about what had happened to the money he had been sending to his mother over the past two years. He looked surprised because they were unaware of any money. Malachi was distrustful of everyone and questioned his uncle about the money and no one knew what he was talking about. Next he questioned the store clerk who had always held contempt for Malachi and his family and found out their landlord was taking the money as payment. This infuriated Malachi and he grew sick in his stomach. He could not believe on top of putting his mother out and showing no mercy he had stolen what little he could afford to send his mother. It was not much but she would not have to worry about eating.

He made arrangements with a neighboring family who happened to be a close friend he had served with so his mother would not have to worry about anything as long as she lived. He made arrangements to pay six dollars a month until he sent word of her death. He vowed to take work close to where she now lived so he could visit as often as possible but first he had something he had to do.

Malachi saddled his horse and rode through the woods contemplating his plan. The closer he rode toward the man who had been so cruel to his family the madder he become. There had not been a time in his entire life he could remember this man ever being nice to them or offering a helping hand. He hated the man almost as much as he hated his father. No one knew what he planned. He felt they were safe if they did not know.

It was about an hour before dark when he reached the edge of the clearing. He stood astounded by what he saw across the well groomed field. A big white house having six large pillars across the front porch stood like tall virgin pine. Several Negro men milled about in the front yard. The dog barked its irritation at the men as it walked toward the smokehouse and disappeared. He spoke to himself careful not to be heard. "What does anyone need with dat big'a house?" Shaking his head he ties his horse to a small cedar tree then pulls his rifle from its sheath. He knew they had an old bloodhound. His first task was to locate him before he was discovered. There next to the smokehouse the old dog was sound asleep, unaware of his presence until the long blade of his knife sank deep into his heart silencing their only alarm to intruder. Malachi will never forget the startled look in the dog's eyes similar to the Indian he killed out on the scrub, but quickly dismissed any thought or feeling of remorse. Reaching down he struggles at first grabbing the back leg of the limp bleeding dog and drug him to the front porch. He tossed him at the top step then retreated back to where he had tied his horse. He knelt in silence keeping a sharp eye on the area around the house until the stillness was broken by the shrill scream of a small child who had discovered the dead dog. An old man bent over at the waist stepped to the porch and kicked at the dead dog. The lifeless body rolled to the ground landing in a brown pile. He straightens up as best he could and stares out into the shadows. Malachi ducks behind the cedar tree fearful the old man saw him because he looked right at him. In the same breath began to cuss. The words roll from his tongue like water being poured from a bucket. The longer he cussed, stomped and spite the louder he became. What he did next infuriated Malachi, he grabbed the little helpless girl by the pony tail spinning her around then knocking her to the ground. Malachi took at deep breath in disbelief and at that moment he knew this man must be dealt with. Without another thought he lifted the rifle to his shoulder taking perfect aim at the man's head now relaxed enough to bend back forward and pulled the trigger. The explosion startled everyone standing around him as they watched the lifeless body of this brutal man tumbled forward landing next to the dog. As Malachi dropped the gun to his side he watched as the little girl stood there splattered with blood whipping her own blood from the corner of her mouth. She stared at her father without any emotion. Most children would have run from the area but not her she just stood there staring. This lack of feeling troubled Malachi more than the actual act of death.

Shapeless forms poured from the house and the surrounding buildings like ants. Each hurried in the direction of the front of the house. Strangely none looked or even offered to head in the direction the shot had come. Malachi shakes his head not understanding what was unfolding before his eyes. The sun now set behind the trees. The darkness was broken only by the few lanterns held in the hands of the curious. Malachi could not be sure but what he figured to be the oldest son bent down, rolled the dead man to his back then stood up and stepped over his father's lifeless body. He seemed uninterested in the dead man and without expression he reached out for his little sister and gathered her up into his arms, holding her close. Malachi was surprised no one was interested in finding the person responsible for the death of their father and master. Or did they even care. The boy handed the child to his mother and everyone watched as he walked to the barn vanishing into the darkness. Malachi's heart began to beat wildly knowing he must leave now but his curiosity caused him to stay and watch. The boy returned carrying only a shovel. He then shouted orders to the Negros standing still wide eyed to drag the body behind the barn and bury him. Before handing them the shovel he sternly instructed them to not mark the grave. Malachi watched the entire incident in amazement. There were no tears for the loss of this man.

The sun was now completely above the horizon as he climbed into the saddle and rode out into the scrub. The sick feeling he had felt when he had killed before was not present. The sickness he felt was for the children who could see their father dead and not feel any emotion. Aimlessly he rode along the well used trail reliving the evening before wondering if having the things this man's family had was worth the indifference he witnessed from the family at his death.

For the next few days he laid low fearing he would be the one everyone would suspect but he never heard another word about the man's death. Two weeks when he visited the family. It was more out of morbid curiosity than anything else. He questioned them as to why there was no investigation into the death but not a word was said other than no one knew what had happened and no one really cared. While visiting the store one afternoon picking up a few supplies for his mother he learned that the land his father had once owned was never transferred from his name and it actually still belonged to his family but would soon be sold for taxes. This angered Malachi even more knowing the cruelty of the man had robbed him of even more than the loss of his father. He sought advice from his regiment commander the only man he truly trusted. Paid the taxes and retook possession of the land. He was able to move his family back onto the land. There were no questions about the disappearance of the mean man who had mysteriously vanished. Life returned to normal.

Malachi found work with a local plantation owner who wanted to expand his holdings by going into the cattle business. Word had drifted north of the lucrative business of shipping cattle to Cuba. This caused him to purchased two hundred and fifty head of cattle from a man west of St. Augustine. Malachi knew the country and was hired to go take charge of the herd and drive the cattle to his place. After out-fitting his self and four free Negros; which all had some knowledge of cattle and they rode west. Lately Malachi had experienced more frequent fevers and the blood he would cough up would sometimes weaken him so he would spend days in bed gathering his strength. He found peace from all of his aches and pains while in the wide open spaces. It was on this trip he concluded driving cattle was what he was made for. One of the greatest memories was when they stopped at a deep creek and just before they crossed they spent the afternoons fishing. He had never witnessed grown men have such fun doing the simplest act of fishing. He got lost in their enthusiasm as he could not help but watch them. Not one of the men he rode with was less than six feet tall but none would take a catfish off their line.

The Negros assigned to this commission was much taller than Malachi and smelt like four old sweaty boar hog on a hot summer day. Their huge frames were scantly clothed. Each was aware of their state in life but did not allow their status to ruin what freedom they enjoyed. Each were born into slavery and worked hard for their personal freedom. One evening as darkness fell Malachi feeling pretty comfortable with the men jokingly told them all they needed a bath. His teasing was met with a persistent assurance, that if he did he fear it would kill the fish in the creek they would all jump in and do just that. To which everyone laughed. The rest of the night was satisfying. Malachi learned he could trust these men. Due to the size of their huge arms they could have easily overpowered him and taken that opportunity to run but they possessed a humility he had never seen in other men and an understanding he had never known before in any other man.

The five of them developed a strong bond and a durable friendship lasting far beyond their working relationship. On the third day of their trip they crossed the St. John's River below the Columbus-Georgia Road. Malachi figured it would be wise and stuck to the thick woods. The going was rough in they had to cut their way through some really thick underbrush. The youngest of the Negros was named Bop and he told Malachi the job of clearing the way would be a lot easier if he could use the big knife he had. Malachi quickly said, "no", because no one but himself ever touches his knife. Malachi feared the fact their small band of misfits could be seen as suspicious. When they finally arrived at what was called cow crossing they were told the cattle they were looking for had not yet been delivered. They had a decision to make, they could either stay around the settlement waiting until the cattle were delivered or head further south. They would try to intercept the herd at Sanderson.

Malachi and the others stood around the large set of holding pens that covered about five acres where he is introduced to a man by the name of Thomas Kinney. This same Thomas Kinney was later appointed by Governor DuVal as the new Superintendent of Indian Affairs for the new State of Florida. He was interested in accompanying Malachi's band of misfits south to Sanderson. Kinney agreed to bare a letter to the man who was holding the cattle informing him the cattle were to be released to Malachi Tanner and his men. It was on this leg of the trip when he got the idea he could make good money as a hunting guide for rich northerners. This would prove to be a source of income for him and his family when times get hard.

After traveling for several hours they stopped and made camp early in the evening. The men busied themselves with preparing the camp. Each of the men was tired because the terrine was thick. Malachi shared in the cutting of the trail. The large knife sliced through the thick briars but the long cane knifes the Negros purchased in Jacksonville made the clearing of the path much easier so Malachi retreated to the back of his horse so he could rest.

After stopping Malachi wanted to slip away from camp and secure some fresh meat. Mr. Kinney asked permission to go. He told Malachi if he was satisfied with the hunt he would pay Malachi ten dollars to which he enthusiastically agreed. Malachi reached down to pick up his rifle motioning for him to follow. Mr. Kinney assured Malachi he would not need his rifle because he was a good shot. Malachi told him he was taking his gun just in case they ran across anything that could harm them, including Indians. Kinney reached out and tugged on Malachi's shoulder turning him to look into his face. He said with a slight smile on his face. "You mean we could see Indians?" Quickly he turned having a concerned and puzzled expression. With wide eyes he looked around. Malachi smiles thinking his shock was rash and assures him he will be safe but needs to keep his eyes open.

The sun was beginning to set as the shadows began to grow long. At that moment Malachi saw a ten-point buck feeding along the edge of a switch-grass pond. Willows grew right in the middle so dense they looked impenetrable. Mosquitoes buzz around the head sounding loudly in his ears. Stinging him furiously causing Mr. Kinney to want to swat but knew better because any quick motion would draw the attention of the feeding buck. The deer disappeared around a myrtle bed so Malachi stood quickly followed by Kinney. He wanted to get another angle when Malachi motioned for him to stop. Like all novice he was not paying attention and run right up Malachi's back. He glared at his companion using his hand in a downward motion indicated he wanted him to stop right there. Turning in the direction of the enormous buck now stopped because something from the opposite direction caught his attention. Instinctively Mr. Kinney lifted his rifle and started to squeeze the trigger when Malachi quickly placed his hand on top of the gun and pushed down. At that instance Mr. Kinney also saw what had captured the deer's attention and caused his shot to be interrupted.

Off in the distance they noticed movement of a rather large band of Indians slipping in the direction of their camp. Falling back they faded back into the brush. Malachi and Mr. Kinney made a small circle hurrying back to camp. Their abrupt entrance into camp startled the resting riders and called for them to follow him. Jumping to their feet they scrambled to break camp and the only evidence of their presence was a single column of smoke rising from the drenched camp fire. He had always been insistent they leave no sign of their presence or any indication of how long they had been gone. Today would have to be different the reason why he did not want to be caught by a raiding party in the wide open with his butt exposed. In a single file they entered the hard wood swamp; which broke into an open cypress strand. The moment Malachi stepped into the opening the needles and dried up ferns made it difficult to move without being heard. With each step the noise echoed. Malachi turned motioning for Mr. Kinney to come close and whispered next to his ear. "There's no way we can all be quite in this strand. I believe they's gonna be just up ahead. Take your men back to where we entered the strand and spread out. Tell yer men to stay hid and quite, I am gonna ease along and see if'n I can find out what they goona do." Malachi then waved for Ezra, when he shuffled forward Malachi told him. "Take the horses back to where we camped and ya'll stay there. If I ain't back fer daylight in the morning yer free to do what ya want. I will be back as soon as I can". With that Malachi turned and disappeared behind a thick stand of myrtles. He knew they would never be able to out maneuver the Indians in the strand so it would be best if he could draw them toward Kinney and his men. Nothing says he cannot try to out-fox the Indians.

Malachi removed his shoes tying them around his neck. Carefully he chose his step not to break any dry branch or limb. Malachi happened upon a small bonnet pond (Lilly pads or lotus) he hoped their adversaries would have to traverse. It wasn't until about an hour after dark as the moon shone bright in the sky as the first Indian entered the small pond. The horses moved slowly ever watchful. Malachi waited as they watched the nerves horses threw their heads up and down. This nervousness caused the rider to be more watchful and on constant alert. Malachi wait until the last rider fully entered the pond to take the first shot. All of a sudden they dismounted and disappeared into the head high palmettos opposite of him.

The eastern horizon looked as if it was on fire. Waves of gray and orange streaked as far as he could see. The brightness hurts Malachi's tired eyes. Daylight only confirmed Malachi's belief. The Indians had the same idea as himself but fortunately for them he saw them first as one stood up to take a leak. Malachi was able to get a few more shots off before they were able too. Bullets wiz by Malachi's head striking the trees behind him and shredding palmettos fans sending a shower of pieces all around him. The shooting stopped as fast as it began. Malachi took this opportunity to turn, drawing the remaining Indians toward Kinney's men. The men with Kinney were better armed than the Indians and more accurate. For just a moment he stopped firing when he heard the thud of a shot striking the man next to him. Before the man fell prostrate he was dead. The stench of warm blood sickened Malachi as he returned fire in the direction of the puffs of smoke from the single shot rifles. He had moved his position affording him a better view of those hiding across the bonnet pond. The once peaceful and lush pond now stained with the blood of man and animal. The shots from that direction are not as many as they once were, declining until there were no more. When the smoke cleared two of Kinney's men lay dead side by side in the shadow of a large oak tree but they were successful in killing all of the Indians. In all of the excitement Malachi began to cough and lost his breath a few times. Standing he stumbles forward hitting the ground with a dull sound sending dust up around his drained body. Thinking he had been shot Kinney ignored the death of his men and rushed to Malachi's side rolling him onto his back. Sweat poured from his face as one of the men kneeled beside him and poured cool water from his canteen onto his brow. He began to calm down and regain his composure. He sits up and asked how long he had been lying there when Kinney stood up reached into his pocket taking out the money he had intended on paying Malachi for the hunt tossing it next to him and said. "Just a minute but you scared the hell out of me".

Two of the Negros hurriedly buried the two unfortunate strangers and off they rode for Sanderson. The rest of the morning as they rode along leaving the small pond and all that had happened farther behind them all Kinney could say was "thank you".

Malachi had never before been to Sanderson. The small settlement could not be missed on the high sandy scrub because of the well used two rut road leading through the dense scrub. It had not rained for several weeks and the air was so hot it was beginning to become difficult for anyone to breath. By mid morning every ones clothes were drenched and their canteens were nigh empty. As they drew closer they could see several columns of smoke rising high into the sky. Unusually large columns, slowly drifting to the west high in the sky, it was then Mr. Kinney told of the turpentine camps. He was a well dressed gentleman who wore a large wide brim hat and rod a large bay horse. Malachi had always thought his fancies were foolishness but he yielded to him, allowing Mr. Kinney to take the lead as they passed by several scruffy looking men sitting on the board walk in front of the only mercantile store. They seemed intently interested in the four Negros following close behind Malachi, they continually made slang comment. No one dare look right at the men because they knew their staring would be interrupted as an act of provocation. Mr. Kinney finally got his belly full of their aggravation, stopping his horse, climbed down and stood side ways to the men. He turned to facing the men revealing the large dragoon hanging on his hip. He smiled a provocative smile and asked if they knew where he could find a man by the name of Koon. His forwardness took the men by surprise causing them to refocus on him rather than the Negro's. This helped to abate a situation everyone knew was coming. The oldest of the men stood, cleared his throat nervously and spoke telling Mr. Kinney he could continue to the end of the road he would see a large set of pens. Sarcastically, he looked at the others and said. "It's wer all da cows is at". His comment caused thunderous laughter. Getting a little braver every moment he went on to say Koon could be recognized by the large straw hat he wore cocked to one side. While they were still laughing Mr. Kinney shot back and said. "Now, the cows you are talking about are they the four footed kind or the two legged butt ugly ones like you?" The look on his face and the sternness of his voice must have hit a nerve because the laughter stopped and the old man coward turned and walked away. Mr. Kinney tipped his hat and thanked the men for the information and ended their conversation by asking his second question about a good place to eat. A toothless old man still standing next to the riders smiled and said if you'll buy some of Koon's cows he'll feed you. With that Mr. Kinney wheeled his horse looking straight at Malachi, smiled and motioned for him to follow. At that moment the sound of several shotguns could be heard un-cocking as the men who looked hostile toward the strangers noticed they were covered by the riders with Mr. Kinney. He looked at Malachi and smiled and said you saved me and I was willing to have those men killed for you.

Kinney rode his horse right in the middle of a conversation Koon was having with some drovers. The men looked weary from weeks on the trail driving a large herd from south Florida. Kinney and Koon walked toward the only café in Sanderson. Due to the late hour Malachi and his companions chose to camp under an oak hammock about a quarter mile from the cow pens. It took that distance to get far enough away from the pens so they did not have to smell the stink. After settling in for the night and the fire burning bright in the darkness several of the drovers from south Florida called out to the fire and were welcomed in. Malachi immediately took a liking to the head drover who was rugged but easy going. He stood about six foot two inches tall and looked just like a scarecrow. His hair looked greasy black with a bushy mustache that covered his mouth. He introduced himself as Jim Lanier. They lived in the Kissimmee River Valley in a small settlement called Crab Grass. The cows belonged to the Yates' and are the best Malachi had seen in a long time. They agreed to share the camp and enjoyed fresh venison, sweet potatoes that cooked in the coals to a tender tasty treat and hot coffee. Malachi listened to Jim as he spoke of the vast open prairies along the St. Johns and Kissimmee Rivers. There were thousands of acres of free grazing and thousands of cows just running free for the taking. If a man did have a desire for cows there were plenty of them rascals for the taking. He told of the tributaries flowing from ceaseless springs just boiling out of the ground and the many high and dry hammock's he had personally seen. He tells of how he intended on moving his family there one day. The game is so abundant. Deer move in large herds, wild hogs root acres at one time. He looked at Malachi and asked if he had ever tasted a banana and Malachi shuck his head no, fascinated and spell bound as Jim described what a banana looked and tasted like. Wild cattle and horses roam everywhere for the taking with very few people. The only problem knew of where the Indian. They just do not understand that we deserve to have some land of our own. The information Jim shared with such enthusiasm and detail peeked Malachi's interest and from what he had personally seen as a scout east of Fort Gatlin he secretly began planning to go south to this land of promise as soon as he could gather enough resources.

Early the next morning they shared another pot of steaming hot coffee and friendly conversation before returning to Sanderson. Mr. Kinney made arrangements for Malachi and his crew to take possession of two hundred and fifty cows, than an additional one hundred head Malachi had purchased from Jim Lanier and also purchased his first brand which happened to be a "T". He took a running iron and added a "1" behind the present brand making the family brand to "T1". The two hundred and fifty cows bore the brand of "ST" that was transferred to the new owner. Even though Malachi had experience in driving cattle he had never done it on the scale of this size. Malachi took this opportunity to learn as much as he could by watching the Negro's as they instinctively work the cattle. Their first big obstacle was crossing the St. John's River. The oldest of the four Negros eased his horse down the bank as it gives way slightly causing a cloud of dust to waft up and around the surefooted horse. The deep water and its current forced the horse to right away to start swim. The cows followed in a single file line through the water and onto the far bank. It took about two hours for the last of the cows to cross the river and for the five men to bring the herd under control. The herd headed west allowing the cows to eat their fill. They were not in a hurry so they moved at their own pace. In the middle of the third week Malachi and the drovers finally entered familiar territory and relieved to see the plantation owner and his foreman ride up and take his first look at his investment. He commented about the additional cows, when Malachi told of his purchase. As they rode along just casually talking when the question was asked what Malachi intended to do with his part of the herd? Malachi spoke frankly and told him he had not honestly thought that far ahead. The plantation owner barked at the four men assigned to Malachi as they were nothing more than the animals they had drove from Sanderson. To being to push the cattle because he wanted them secure in his pasture before dark. Than looking at Malachi he said follow me and spurring his horse they galloped toward the main gate. This was the first time he had actually had an opportunity to consider what he would do with his part of the cows but agreement was made to allow them to stay with the other for the next few weeks.

Malachi stayed one more night and at the insistence of the plantation owner he stayed in one of his spare rooms. The next morning he met with the friends he had made while on the trip and promised to see them again. As they spoke together the plantation owner walked up and in his arrogance acknowledged no one but Malachi and asked what he paid for his cows. Surprised by the question he told him he paid four dollars a head. Now standing with his hands on his hips the plantation owners offered Malachi double of what he paid in cash. He looked off toward the feeding cows and turned to the four black men that had faded into the shadow of their conversation and asked. "How much are these men's life worth to you?" He looked taken aback by the question and he said. "They ani't worth one hundred cows if that's what yer asken". Malachi looked at him inquisitively awaiting a response when he asked trying hard to understand what Malachi was getting at. "You want to trade one hundred head of cows for four wore out old Negros?" Without a hesitation Malachi answered yes. To which the plantation owner quickly stuck out his hand offering it to him as a sign of the contract. Malachi looked at the men standing there and all he could see were the wipe smiles across their faces. Malachi stepped into the saddle and told them. "Let's go we got a long way to go". They hurried to their cabin gathered what little they owned and trotted after their new young master.

Once they were out of sight of the plantation Malachi dismounted and walked with his new found friends in silence. The Negros had never been treated like equals and because of that they were distrustful toward Malachi. He noticed them speaking among themselves when he heard the severe scolding of Ezra toward the others causing them to cow down. Sheepishly they followed without saying another word. After traveling about twenty miles the sun began to set behind the tall pine trees. Malachi reached for his rifle than handed it to the man closes to him and asked if he would see if he could shot them some fresh meat. Without thought he grabbed the gun than looked at the other men with a confused look on his face as if asking what he should do. Then he looked back at Malachi who simple smiled and told him he did not want to eat coon. His expression told a story of mistrust and a deep embedded prejudice against any white man no matter if they are good to them or not. Malachi figured this was as good a time to tell him his intentions. He tied his horse to a low branch of a scrub oak just off the trail and called for the men to follow him. Without a thought he turned into a small scrub oak thicket finding a big enough place for them to make camp. They sat and stared at Malachi when he finally spoke. "You're free to go and do whatever you like." Their mouths dropped open and with wide eyes they looked at each other. Before they could respond to what he was saying he continued. "If I were you though, I would head south into Florida. I hear you can join the Indians and live like real men without any limits." Malachi stood up and headed back toward where he tied his horse. Just before disappearing into the thicket he turned and said. "Now let's gather some fire wood while you go gets us some meat." Malachi heads toward a small open patch among the pines and gathers an armful of small pieces of lightered. Turning back toward the camp he notices that three of the Negros were are gone. The only one left was Ole Ezra when it dawned on him that one of the young bucks took his rifle. What would he do if he had to replace it? Disbelief and anger swells within him as he tosses the lightered down where he intended to build the fire. After a few minutes Malachi tried to figure a way to properly express his feelings without sounding like he was accusing the young man of stealing. Taking a meaningful breath then looked inquisitively at the old man and demanded, "Where the hells my gun?" Slowly the old man explained, "Two of the boys went back to the creek to fetch water and to wash up. They say they will gather more wood for the fire on the way back. The other figured it wouldn't take him long to kill something and be back." Malachi was relieved yet a little embarrassed in thinking they had run off the first chance they got. For this he learned to respect them more as men than just the deep rooted belief they are the property of another.

That night as they ate fresh venison grilled over an open fire along with steaming hot sweet potatoes the youngest of the men asked if Malachi was being truthful when he said they were free. Malachi assured them their debt had been paid and they were as free as he. Again he warned them that as long as they stayed around here even though they were free some men will always consider them as the property of another. They need to think hard about heading south into Florida. As Malachi spoke he could see the young man relax. The furrowed angry brow now took on a peaceful look taking a stick in his hand he poked the fire sending ambers of orange and red into the sky. The ambers floating upward mesmerized Malachi as he felt the tension of a life time disappear as the ambers. Lost in the moment he did not hear what the man had to say the first time he spoke. Realizing it was to him he was speaking he lifted his eyes and they met the eyes of the one asking the question. Malachi apologies for not listening and asked if he would repeat the question. "You says I's free, right". Malachi answers yes and asked why he did not believe him when he first said it? The man begins to speak again and everyone became captivated by his story. "I's was born to a free mother. One day while we's were traveling to visit my grandparents a man stopped our wagon and raped my mother. I along with my four brothers was forced to watch this man do bad things to our mother." Malachi noticed the crease return to his forehead and his eyes began to narrow. By the flickering of the fire he could see the sweat roll from the defined muscles on his forearms and the clinching of his fist. "My oldest brother, he was only fifteen years old in a fit of rage run toward the man as he got up from on top of my mother and was shot dead. My mother was left for dead. I have no idea if she is still alive but he took us to Savannah and sold us to a farmer. I was separated from my brothers." A single tear rolls down his cheek as it caught the reflection of the lightered fire. Sound of snuffing could be heard as he continued. "I's wants to head north and see if I can find my mother. I's figured I's would travel at night and sleep during the day. It took me two weeks to walk here from Savannah and we lived two day beyond that. I's gonna see if I can find my momma, if not I's gonna head north. Cause people don't hate Negro were up there like they do down here." His resolve convinced Malachi that no amount of persuasion could change his mind. Malachi told him they would stay here for a couple of days as they cooked meat for his trip. He assured him he would help him with as much supplies as he could spare. A big smile flashed across his face as he looked at the other for their approval of his plan.

The mood was light for the next few days. Malachi became anxious about leaving. Fidgety does not describe the atmosphere the last morning they would spend together as a rag tag band. The sun sat as every other night as the moon light flooded the scrub. That evening all but Ezra faded into the night never to be seen again.

Chapter 6

Malachi was able to purchase two extra long legged boney horses. One was given to Ezra to ride and the other will be use as a pack horse. Neither men knew how to properly pack a horse but it was a hard lesson both learned real fast. The horse still had a lot of life left in him. You would have thought Ezra was given a golden horse they way he spoke. He just kept repeating. "He had never owned anything like it before." Malachi could not understand his excitement over a sick horse that looked like a piece of skin stretched over bones. Ezra did not care what it looked like he was just proud it was his to keep and no one could take it from him. He would not stop thanking Malachi for the gift. Day by day as the slowly made their way south the horses began to gain weight and look a lot better. Each was extremely glad they did not have to learn to pack a horse while he felt good.

Both men rode south on the Old Coffee Road meandering in and around the dense woods of this strange but familiar land. Black jack's and scrub oaks spotted the high white sandy ridge. Strange pointy bushes if not avoided would drive their hard sharp ends deep into the men's legs. They were so thick Malachi and his party had to get off their horse to lead them. Using the large knife they would cut through vines thicker than a spoon handle with thorns sturdy enough to rip through their tattered pants. Sweat poured from their brow flooding their eyes causing them to burn from the salt. The water was rapidly diminishing and they were in a desperate search for more. Malachi noticed his large knife getting dull and needed tending to soon. About an hour after noon and only having traveled a half of a mile he started feeling weak. He started to dry heave and his head spun like a top. Ezra commented on how Malachi looked so pale and suggested they stop for a few hours so he could rest. He insisted they continue when all of sudden he went limp passing out. He slumped forward onto the thick vines causing the long thorns to rip into his skin, blood gushed from the cuts. Ezra hurried to where he fell, lifting his clammy wet body from off the thorns alarmed at how much he weighted and how frail he was. He carefully carried Malachi the hundred yards back to where the horses were tied. The horses seemed spooked by the large negro carrying a strange form, to which he spoke gently to them and the immediately calmed down but curiously watched what was happening. Lying him down in the shade of a scrub oak tree he poured what little cool water they had onto his forehead trying to break the fever that suddenly engulfed his body. He shivered violently as he began to cough forcefully, spitting up handfuls of blood. Again he passes out. Using his large hand he tried to funnel water into his mouth. Quickly Malachi woke and begun to cough hard, blood still stained his lips trickling down the side of his mouth. He was so weak but he managed to mouth the word, "saddlebag". Ezra hurried to his horse and returned with a small brown bottle containing a black looking liquid with strong pungent smell and a blood stained quilt. Lifting him to a sitting position Ezra managed to pour the fowl smelling tar-like fluid into his mouth. He choked almost incoherent but managed to swallow all of it. Instantly he fell into a deep sleep and slept for three days. Ezra did not want to leave Malachi's side but he did manage to cut the rest of the path through the thick underbrush out into the scrub and find fresh water.

As the sun rose on the fourth day Malachi came too and asked for the bottle of medicine which allowed him to sleep so comfortably. Ezra fetched the bottle from the saddlebags handing it to him. He turned it up taking a long swig. The grimacing expression told the story of the repulsive flavor and repulsive stink Ezra had experienced days before. They camped for several more days as Malachi's strength returned slowly. Ezra managed to kill a rabbit and made a stew with some wild onions he found along the way. He ate eagerly to the last drop passing the small wooden bowl back to Ezra and asked how long he had been out. The old Negro told him he had lost count, than, sheepishly admitting he did not really know because he never learned to count, but he thought it to be about a week. Malachi sat up realizing that he had soiled himself. Embarrassed and shakily he made his way to the small creek thankful Ezra had moved the camp closer. Returning Ezra took note of the fragile frame of his young companion as he unsteadily leaning on a tree dressing his self. Throwing his old clothes aside he lay back down before he passed out and went fast asleep. He woke only once to see the old man had washed his clothes, embarrassed but thankful he watched the flickering of the fire as it danced to the influence of the wind until he feel back asleep.

The next day at the first sign of morning as the light breaks streaking across the scrub. A slight breeze blew and its coolness caused Malachi to shudder letting him know he still was not completely over the episode. He stands rubbing the sleep from his eyes and cannot remember another night he had slept so peaceful. He looked at Ezra and said. "I think we will be able to leave first thing tomorrow morning." To which Ezra said he believed that would be fine. After resting for a bit more he was able to walk to the creek and cool his still sweating brow. He believed this area to be as beautiful as the big creek he first discovered while stationed at Fort Gatlin. The day was restful and needed. The sun sat without incident and after they had enjoyed some grilled pork Malachi retired and slept without waking once.

The moon now full and shone bright against the blue-gray cloudless sky. Other than the chirping of the crickets and the morning dove cooing its dejected cry life seemed to be peaceful. He sits in his bed silently listening to the hush of the night drawing strength for the day ahead. A ritual he had enjoyed and practiced since a little boy. The only thing different now is the sickness seemed to come more frequent and last longer each time. Deep inside Malachi believes one day he would not recover and possibly die by himself out in the wilderness.

The sun now reflects off the droplets of dew hanging on the wire grass and spider webs. Glimmering drops like diamonds flash the brilliant light of the morning sun. Malachi takes as deep of breath as he dares not wanting to start a reaction of intense coughing but to enjoy this new day he has been granted. Off in the distance he hears the last of the sentry call of an old hoot owl just before it retreats to its hiding place among the large live oak trees. The lonely cry only reminds Malachi of the distance he yet has to travel before he can finally rest. He takes another deep breath enjoying the smells and fragrances of a new day. He turns at the first sound of the hissing as the coffee pot boils over spilling small splashes of the hot black liquid trying desperately to douse the flames. The fat back sizzles and crack as the heat from the fire begins to cook their breakfast.

After reaching the Suwannee River they followed the current as it flows west happening by chance on a river crossing called by the locals, Rock

Bluff Ferry. The banks are high covered with hickory, bay and magnolia trees and formations of rock jetting out over the water. Small springs bobble from under the rock running down and the clear water disappears into the brown tannic water. Years of use had carved out a small path down to a small wooden platform extending out over the water. You could almost see the strong current pull and push against the straining timbers of the platform. Stubborn as the man who ran the ferry, Malachi was sure that if he ever pasted this way again he would find this same struggle. Tied to the opposite side of the swift running river is a ferry but there is no one around. Usually Malachi would not pay to cross no river but today he felt it would be best. He would use this time to ask for information to cover his real motive. Ezra called out, his raspy voice echoed off the large trees on the opposite side. He was quickly answered by someone up the other bank. He hollered. "I'll be there directly. I'm busy." Soon they saw a young man emerge from a clump of palmettos adjusting his suspender. The fare was announced before the trip across and agreed to. The steady sloshing of the water as it slapped against the side of the ferry was comforting to Malachi for some reason beyond his understanding.

Once on the other side they traveled a well defined military trial leading due south all the way to Fort Fanning. Fort Fanning sat atop a high bank on the east side of the river on a long sweeping curve. They noticed another ferry and a sign pointing across the river indication the way to Perry and Tallahassee.

They camped for the night at Fort Fanning and purchased the supplies he figured they would need for the remaining trip. While Malachi was in the small store he purchased a sketching pad and several pencils. Trivial possessions but something he enjoyed. Along the way he found it easy to relax while sketching the breath taking landscape. The beauty of the towering water oaks and massive cypress trees decorated by the greenish-gray moss and the red flowering air-plants became his favorite subject. The cherry plum trees were full of their sweet but sour fruit and the fox grapes were so plentiful they hung almost to the ground. Ezra commented as to this being paradise when Malachi reminded him that it still gets really cold here. Thick stands of cedar and cabbage palms shooting high into the sky, the odd shapes of the trunks captured his imagination wondering how long they had grown like that. He remembers while on one of his trips earlier an old man told him that the cabbage trees take about sixty or so years to get that tall. They spent two nights and days at an abandoned Indian camp where he found the sweetest oranges he had ever tasted. If he had not already decided on the big creek he would definitely be satisfied with the seclusion of this place. Returning to the fort to pick up the supplies he had ordered just days before.

He spent the next few weeks at Fort Fanning to regain the strength he lost from traveling alone and living exposed to the unforgiving elements. A local cattleman and hunters will trail a sizable herd to Paine's Prairie for fattening. He had also agreed to allow several ox drawn wagons to follow along as far as the prairie when he will point them in the direction of Micanopy. Malachi noticed a woman as she watched him and whispered to other in their party. There was a strange familiarity about her but he felt uncomfortable in the way she continued to stare. That night after everyone worked together in preparing the site chose for their camp the adults sat next to the fire listening to the low of the cattle as they settle in for the night. Between the lowing of the cattle a lone whippoorwill continued its call until one of its own kind reciprocated. Then they were serenaded until the breaking of a new day. At breakfast the next morning the woman walked up to Malachi and asked him if he had any family of which he answered, "No". He thought she was referring to his dead father, but later he would learn she was talking about brothers and sisters.

About a day into the trek Malachi became captivated by the skill of the hunter and sought employment and was readily hired. They would not allow Ezra to work but he was tolerated because everyone believed he belonged to Malachi. He attentively watched every action of the men working the cattle in order to learn all he could. The yellow deer flies buzz around his ears aggravating him causing him to incessantly slap. At times he would hit himself so hard on the side of his head his ears rang. Some of the hunters notice Malachi and wonders if he was a little touched in the head by the way he slapped his biting enemy. The mosquitoes stung him over his entire body making even his joints ache. Three weeks after joining the drive the terrain began to change. The pine trees towered high above the palmettos along with the occasional stand of oak trees. The gal-berry flats inter-twined with huckleberry, wild blueberries, broom-sage and a verity of yellow and purple flowering plants were replaced by cedars, bay trees and magnolias. Large areas were covered with what Malachi learned were dog fennels. In the hard wood swamp the pungent aroma produced by the huge white flower of the magnolia tree was so present it sickened Malachi due to its sweetness. He was relieved when they finally entered the open expanse of prairie. The wind was not hindered by the waist high grasses as they sway almost touching the ground and then standing again.

The grass so lush and filled with the nutrients needed to strengthen the weakened cows. This helped the cows in having their calves along with helping to produce enough milk giving their young a good chance to make it.

Just before dark, in the middle of the week Malachi saw a few Indians. He was captivated by the bright color of their clothing. He settled next to a large bay tree in order to sketch a picture of a people that seemed to be nothing more than abrasions until they sweep in and attack. One of the older hunters named Jim Cotton followed Malachi and when he spoke it startled him making him flinch. Jim had an empty stare and it told of his hatred for the Indians. Malachi was confused and did not understand until he told his story.

"We first came to Florida in thirty-four. During the second week of our four week trip to Fort Defiance and Fort McCoy the Indians struck fast and hard. I should have been more alert but the going was ruff and I put all of my attention in cutting a big enough trail to safely pass". He stares into nowhere when Jim spoke matter-of-fact and continued. "Have you ever seen a chicken hawk fly down and catch a chicken?" Taking a step forward he gets right in Malachi's face. "That's how they did. A small band of, I think six of those red bastards swept in without warning killing my two youngest girls. I had to watch helplessly as they beat them to death. I hate'em. They struck without mercy and before the dust could even settle they drove off one of my best ox." Malachi could see in Jim's face distorted with grief etched with fury. "We could see the glow of the fire used to cook the stolen ox. All night long we had to listen to their whooping and hollering. Hatred grew that night inside me for those savages." He looked with a narrowing expression and told how he quickly buried their broken bodies trying hard to comfort his wife now blaming him indirectly for their death.

"The way got harder and took longer because we only had three oxen to pull the two wagons. Somewhere out on that scrub we had to abandon most of the furniture we had brought from Georgia. For almost a week those savages paralleled us. I took several shots at them but they just faded into the woods. At night they just screamed and by the forth night my wife could not take it anymore taking my old pistol she killed herself. Those bastards waited until we entered a clearing when they struck again. I managed to kill the first two as they rushed in over confident. The others over powered me and tied me to a nearby tree. They made me watch as they raped and murdered my oldest girl." He gagged as he said. "She was only eleven years old. They then beat the three boy's unconscious and leaving them for dead as they drove off the other three oxen. I remained tied until late the next day when my eldest son finally woke from his beating. He struggled to his feet complaining he was very sore and I could see blood rolling from an open gash in his head. He managed to crawl to where I was and untie me then fell to the ground. I gathered what supplies not destroyed and tended to my injured children but with all my effort only two survived. By then I had dug my fifth grave and vowed that if it was in my power I will never bury another of my children." He looked straight into Malachi eyes and he shivered at the coolness telling him of his hatred of every Indian with a passion as he lifts his rifle to his shoulder and without warning pulls the trigger. Malachi turns in time to see the lead Indian falls from his horse as if in slow motion. Within seconds there were at least twelve riders atop dancing horses asking what was happening, when Jim stood he said. "A damned Indian." Then he pointed across the open flat. All at once several shots echoed across the open scrub followed by the war cry of charging Indians as Jim stumbled forward. He had a look of disbelief as blood stained his shirt. Malachi will never forget the look on Jim's face as he topples forward dead before he hit the ground. In unison the hunters bolted in the direction Jim had pointed just before he fell in determined pursuit of those Indians who had gotten away. Malachi could not believe what he was witnessing as he scrambled to his feet replacing his sketch pad with his rifle, mounted his horse and rode back toward the herd. Malachi will not be a part of senseless killing. He waited at camp still hearing the echo of rifle shots across the scrub. The next morning while the hunters were receiving their assignments Malachi saddled his horse. After gathering his belongings he untied the reins noticing he needed to soon replace the weathered leather reins. He led his horse toward where the other men were standing and watched the reaction of each as they curiously spoke among themselves questioning what he was doing. Stopping next to where Mr. Blackburn stood he announced he was leaving. Mr. Blackburn was a man of few words and seemed a little irritated at this development. He spoke short telling Malachi he was unable to pay all he agreed because he was not accustomed to carrying paper money with him while on the trail but he could have what he had. Malachi simple shook his head acknowledging what he told him letting him know he did not care about the money and he could do with it what he wanted.

CHAPTER 7

1892

On the other side of the dry pond each step he took small billows of dust rose up around his feet. He could not believe the rain of several days ago was now dried up and gone. Malachi continued due east following an old game trail for about an hour when he saw the first sign of a wagon as it cut deep ruts in the white sandy bottom. Fresh cut grapevines crunch under his feet when he noticed two sets of footprints over the top of the ruts. He pulls back on the reins of his horse and surveys the horizon. Off in the distance he caught movement and the first glimpse of a wagon recognizing it as the one that had also separated from Mr. Blackburn's company several days before. Malachi figure since there was so much Indian activity it would be safer to join them but unsure if he would be welcome. They were so occupied with cutting a wide enough trail for the wagon they never noticed him approaching from their rear. Malachi shouted out to the man off to one side causing him to drop to one knee quickly aiming his long rifle in Malachi's direction. Raising his hand in the air indicating he meant no harm carefully walked his horse up beside the man and introduced his self. Malachi could not help but stare at the wagon loaded with what little possessions they had in this world. Malachi recognized him as Bass Thompson. He seemed to be relieved with the presence of another man who could help if there will be any trouble. He hesitated for a moment looking toward where his wife as she washed the last of the morning dishes. Just then Malachi saw her for the first time. Honestly up to that moment he had no idea she was on the trip. The girl stood five feet three inches tall, her hair jet black and flowed down around her shoulders. She wore a faded blue dress. It could not conceal the fact that she was a young woman revealing every curve of her sun tanned body. He had never seen anyone or anything as beautiful. Malachi was unaware of anything until Mr. Thompson touched the lower part of his leg causing him to jump. He apologized to him and to his wife for his forwardness still unable to take his eyes off of the beautiful young girl now smiling back at him. Malachi's heart fluttered almost taking his breath away.

Her father finally spoke inhospitably saying even though they could use his help but he did not believe it to be a good idea for him to travel with them because of the circumstances. No one had noticed Mrs. Thompson as she walked up next to the wagon and listened to their conversation. He spoke at last and assured Mr. Thompson he could be trusted and he would be good help if they happened across any Indians. With that he turned to Malachi and whispered. "Don't make me have to talk to you. I have enough problems without you causing more." Malachi guaranteed him he had not made a mistake assuring him his intentions were as pure as the young woman herself.

He mounted his horse and rode off in an eastern direction toward the rising sun. All he could think about was the young woman that rode in the wagon behind him. He began to doubt himself wondering if any woman could find him attractive because of his small frame and his sickness. Could anyone love him when he was coughing up blood and unable to carry on the daily chores of life? With anger brewing in his chest he quickly dismissed any thought of her and focused on the trail before them. The first obstacle was a deep clear fast flowing river. Along the well defined bordered of the river stood tall cabbage trees, towering sixty feet high into the sky. It was the time of year when the cabbage berries fell to the ground. Birds flew from one top to another filling the belly with the ripe fruit. Cedar trees and live oak trees grew only half the height of the cabbages. Pokeberry bushes, small clumps of palmettos spotted along a well traveled path, a few low growing pine trees and bay trees crowd the way. These brush up next to the wagon drawing the attention of the young woman as she peers around the back of the wagon when her eyes met Malachi's and she smiles. Her eyes sparkle catching the rays of the sun sending shivers down his spine intoxicating him with thoughts he had never known before. His heart beat harder than the time he killed his first man. He knees almost buckled. Suddenly he turns from her stare not wanting her or her father to think him too forward. Spurring the horse forward it bolts toward and jumping into a small clump of palmettos. Malachi wanted a place where he could hide and clear his mind. The horse danced around wondering what was wrong with its rider. He took a deep breath and for the first time it did not hurt or cause him to cough.

The rest of the day was hot and filled with tiring work. While clearing an open path for the wagon he was able to forget about his embarrassing action. The girl watched each step and action Malachi took. Just before the noon meal he noticed her looking at him, this helped to energies him giving him his second wind. He could have swung the large knife forever and by the end of the day every muscle burned.

The long shadows of the last beams of light swept across the ground as Mr. Thompson rode next to where he stood and told him they could stop and make camp. Relieved by the announcement he collapsed to the ground forgetting about his pride.

Not ready to see her again he saddles the horse and rides further south scouting for an easier way. While there he would kill some fresh meat for their supper. They moved in opposite directions. Time got away from Malachi as he rode aimlessly, his mind thinking of every possible thing that could happen this first night together.

The moon was now high in the shy causing shadows. Malachi rode watchful along the river when he happened upon a ford in the river. This allowed him time to clear his head and form an acceptable excuse for his absence. On his way back to the place they would camp for the night he saw a small maiden doe. Killing it he returned to camp with his wallet filled with tender back strap. Stopping at the edge of the camp he surveyed the area and could not see her. As he rode up he could hear splashing and laughing coming from the direction of the river. Curiously he looked through the thick brush and there just a few feet from the bank he saw her naked pale body illuminated by the moonlight. She sees him at the same time he became aware of what he was seeing and blushes. She slowly drops to her knees underneath the surface of the water and swam away from his view as he turns and rides away. That night at supper it was Malachi who was careful not to allow their eyes to meet because he did not know if she took offence at his watching her or not. He was not willing to take that chance. Her response to his actions was more offensive and she told him so. She made it clear to him she knew what she was doing and if she did not want him to notice her she would have bathed further down the river. Before she stomped away from the fire to the back of the wagon for the night she kissed him on the cheek. Her actions caused Malachi to blush again. A devilish smile crossed his face to which her father stood demanding to know what was going on. Malachi, with a dumbfounded look on his face simply shrugged his shoulders in silent defiance. Mr. Thompson still standing waiting for an explanation when the girl's mother walked to where he stood whispering something into his ear, to which he turned and walked into the darkness. Malachi's heart beat so fast and so loud he was afraid no one would get any rest in the camp and wondering if he should just pack up his stuff and leave. He was so confused and lay in his bedroll watching the fire and lost track of time. Startled by rustling in the bushes behind him he turns, there standing in the shadows was her father. Without a word he sits next to Malachi and throws another piece of lightered wood on the fading fire. They sat in silence for a few minutes when he finally spoke up asking Malachi to please wait until they were married to do anything. He blushingly admitted his daughter was head strong and was going to do what she wanted because she was just like her mother. He went on to say that same trait was what drew him to her mother. Malachi could sense the man begin to relax and very talkative. Malachi now was really befuddled at last spoke and said. "I don't even know her name." The man looked surprised at his declaration and kind of chuckled and said, "Mollie." Turning back toward the fire he repeated. "Mollie, her name is Mollie. She's a hard-headed and strong willed girl. That is one reason we are on this trip. I don't want ya to think she's a bad girl, she's not. I just want better fer her than what was in Georgia." With that he stood, stretched looking around than walked toward the small canvas tent mumbling. Malachi's first thought was to pack up right then and ride away as fast as he could. But the threat of Indians was still present and to leave would put both he and this family at risk if they were discovered.

CHAPTER 8

1893

After five weeks of steady traveling, the drudgery of the terrain and the hypnotic squeaking of the wheels as they turned round and round became unbearable at times. The only thing that broke up this repetitiveness was the occasional gopher hole that jarred the wagon and its occupants.

A particular day would begin way before daylight with the preparation of a meager meal. Usually left over from the night before, that is if the weather was so hot it did not spoil. The blow flies at times were so numerous at times they could not even eat without their aggravation. Rain was a exacting foe to Malachi and his soon to be wife and her family.

Early one morning the clouds grew dark and off in the distance the thunder rumbled like a stampeding herd of wild cattle. The flashes of lightening grew more intense forcing them to take refuge in a small oak hammock. The largest of the oaks offered shelter because it had fallen over sometime in the past making a natural haven. By simply removing one limb they were able to back the wagon in under the massive limbs. Just as they had draped the large canvas over the back of the wagon and into the limbs the first large rain drops began to fall. It rained hard for the rest of the day and late into the night. There was nothing to do but sit and watch the small streams of rain water as it washes across the ground. He found pleasure in lifting the canvas causing the water to pond on top and sag filling the drinking barrels. Malachi became restless just sitting around doing nothing and decided when morning came he would get out and explore. The women folk slept in the wagon and the men dug trenches around a raised area next to the fire that had a slight fall to insure the water run away from their bed roll. This was the first time Malachi was able to stay high and dry during a rain like this for as long as he could remember. The rain let up and stayed at a steady drizzle until noon the next day. At daylight the next day the rain stopped for about an hour allowing Malachi to gather several large lightered logs to insure a good supply of dry wood for warmth and cooking. While out he killed a she coon and this provided a tasty stew.

After spending two miserable days at this camp they were finally able to pack up and start moving south again. The small trail they were traveling was littered with fallen trees making the going more difficult. Mollie's mother had become sick during the rain and contributed to the delay as well. Mister Thompson and Malachi used the cross saw and chopped the fallen trees for the next several days until they were able to enter a scrub not affected by the storm. Every day they were challenged and every time it was met with a determination. Both men would not allow this harsh wilderness to discourage them. Both were struck by the beauty of the land and grew to depend on each other.

They were able to make about five miles a day through the thick pine flat. When they entered the high sandy scrub even if they did not exert much energy they were able to make ten to twelve miles in a single day. The first creek they came to was swollen and very precarious to cross. Mr. Thompson unhooked the oxen from the wagon and allowed them to feed on the lush grasses growing alongside the creek bottom. Taking hold of a long stretch of rope he carefully picked his way across the creek. Using a pulley he had brought along securing it to a large pine tree. He marveled at the massive pines that grew up to sixty feet high. Running the length of rope through the pulley he crossed back across tying one end to the wagon and the other to the yoke on the oxen he was able to guide the wagon to the other side without much effort. He and Malachi then made their way back across the creek each leading an ox. Once on the other side they decided to camp for a few days to allow the oxen to rest and eat the grasses to regain their strength they had so faithfully lost leading the family this far. While camp was being set up Malachi and Mollie was given permission to go out into the scrub where Malachi helped her to kill her first deer. That night Mollie and her mother sat up next to the fire and when they thought Malachi was asleep Mollie talked of how much she liked him. She told her mother she wanted to spend the rest of her life with him. Her mother listened patiently trying hard to discourage her because she knew Malachi wanted to live in the back woods and life would be hard. There was no amount of persuasion that would change Mollie's mind. She was determined to live with him no matter how hard life would be. This conversation scared Malachi, realizing she was the first person he was actually afraid of.

The next morning the camp was filled with the smell of coffee boiling next to the fire. This seemed to make the mood of the camp lighter. After hearing the conversation the night before Malachi sensed a change in Mollie's mother and tried hard to prove to her he would be able to take care of her daughter. Everything he would do just irritated her when finally he just gave up. This was his first experience trying and failing to understand a woman. Bass could see his frustration and just laughed.

The sun was already up high in the sky when they finally began to move away from the river bottom. With each step the dense shadows of the swamp faded behind and the sandy ridge with its open spaces grew drier and thicker. The oxen struggled under the weight of the wagon so Mollie and her mother climbed down out of the wagon and walked. There came a time when Malachi had to use his horse tying it in front of the oxen and this offered a little help.

At long last they began a visible descent; into another bottom. Finally they had arrived at the St. Johns River. The cabbage trees towered high into the sky. The temperature dropped several degrees; which was a welcomed sight. There was a small cut trail along the west side of the river leading in and out and around massive cedar trees bigger than any Malachi had ever seen. By chance they happened across a large growth of guavas. The smell was so strong Mrs. Thompson would not eat them. While picking the yellow fruit they jumped several hogs. Malachi was able to shot one that was fat. That night they rendered the fat for lard. Fresh cooked pork over and open fire and the strangely sweet taste of the guava was a feast no one could imagine could come from such a wild place. Bass drank the last of the shine and began to become louder and louder as he shared his excitement and new found confidence he had made the right choice in leaving Georgia. Malachi knew times could get hard here but did not want to spoil his dream.

After traveling several more days they came across a ferry at a cross road. After talking to the ferryman there was a lot of discussion about wanting to cross here and head toward the coast or continue south along the river. Malachi's mind was already made up he wanted to head south toward Fort Reed but he was willing to listen to any argument before offering his option. After talking to the family operating the ferry again Mr. Thompson decided to continue on their present course south.

The man running the ferry insisted they stay a couple of days because it was not often his wife had the company of womenfolk and he really wanted to have some male conversation himself. They had two grown sons who ran a moon-shine still along a small creek north of the ferry and offered some of what they call the best shine around. Malachi did not like the way the shine made him feel so he declined but Mr. Thompson gratefully accepted their invitation. Two days were wasted there and they ended up staying a week. Mrs. Thompson did not like that her husband spending as much time at the still. But she really enjoyed her time visiting Mrs. Cotton. Malachi became restless and insisted they head on and for the first time Mrs. Thompson agreed. After saying their good-byes and Mr. Thompson loading a few jugs of shine into the back of the wagon they headed out. They traveled for several more days. About noon the third day they got their first sight of the big lake. It was larger than any of them had seen. It was decided to camp here for the next few nights and it turned cold. The wind coming across the lake blew hard. The canvas used for their tent whipped and potted. One night Malachi watched from the warmth of his quilt as the fire danced to the rhythm of the wind waiting any moment for the canvas to rip loose but the cypress poles held. That morning was the last of the cold weather for several weeks. Malachi and Mollie enjoyed their time together fishing and hunting. Malachi was amazed by the fact that she seemed to love the wilderness just as much as he did.

Malachi learned by watching what makes a woman happy and what makes a man happy. The lesson he learned was if the women is happy the man is happy.

Each day it was the same up at first daylight and in bed just after dark. The mood in the camp lightened as the heat of the days began to be washed by the cool breeze from the northwest. Mrs. Thompson had several flare ups from her sickness she contracted during the rain several weeks early and caused the trip to take longer than they had anticipated. One night while camping on the high bank of the river a small band of migrating Indians entered the camp in a nonthreatening way. They shared their fire when the old man asked about Mr. Thompson's wife and her sickness. Early the next morning the two Indian women left the camp and soon returned with a small deer skin bag filled with plants and herbs they had gathered while away. They busied themselves around the fire and everyone watched curiously as the ground and boiled a strong smelling black brew. They handed it to Mr. Thompson and instructed him on how his wife was to drink this every night before she was to sleep, it would help her to get over her sickness. Giving her some she was able to finally to sleep. Mollie asked her father if the two Indian women could show her these plants and herbs to which they readily agreed. Mollie spent the rest of the morning with the two women along the river bottom learning from them. There was a language barrier but Mollie learned fast. While the women gathered the plants and herb and Mrs. Thompson slept the men fished. Malachi enjoyed himself more during this unexpected delay then anytime on this trip. That night they enjoyed a feast of fish and swamp cabbage. Bass Thompson pulled out one of the jugs he had gotten several weeks before. The first sight of the jug surprised their visitors. The oldest Indian refused the strong drink and explained how his two oldest sons found the strong drink and it killed them. Tears and a faraway look filled his eyes as he told his story.

The next morning their visitors were gone and Mrs. Thompson was strong enough to travel. It took a few more weeks when they finally ambled up into a settlement by the name of Longwood. It was on a side trail leading between Fort Gatlin where Malachi had spent much of his time while stationed here in the Florida wilderness and Fort Mellon (now known as Sanford, Florida). Malachi was shocked to see a lot more families here than he would have imagined or liked. He longed to return to the big creek he had visited two years before. He could not get the images of the tall sprawling oak hammock in the midst of the virgin pine towering high into the sky. Cabbage trees filled with birds and squirrels. The squirrels were much smaller here in Florida than the ones around his childhood home. The creek continually flowed was filled with fish. To the east of the hammock was a deep clear lake surrounded by cypress trees so large he figured it would take at least six men with their arms out stretched to reach around the massive trees! In his mind he had already fell enough to construct a small cabin for he and Mollie. Malachi wanted Mollie to see the creek but held his tongue because he knew this was not the right time. It had been a long time since he last experienced this feeling of excitement but the harshness of his life had disciplined him to a point he would not show it. This irritated his mother and she had told him of it several times but realized it was not worth bringing it up anymore so she just made up her mind to just stay annoyed. His brothers knew no different. They secretly thought he was a hard man but anyone who truly took the time to know him learned he was compassionate just afraid to open up to anyone.

He visited Fort Mellon and spoke to the captain in charge. Reaching into his front shirt pocket then handing them to the man behind the small unsteady desk showing his papers from where he had served earlier. Immediately he was interested in what Malachi knew. While there he learning a small band of Seminole Indians was causing a little trouble south of Fort Gatlin. They were a small band of Seminoles lead by a renegade from Osceola's band. Secretly Malachi smiles because he had an upper hand in this struggle. His grandmother was sister to Osceola and had spent some time with his band as a child. She had given him a small signet that identified him and his connection with the Seminoles. He had used it on one occasion unaware when he was leading a few men between Fort Defiance and Fort McCoy. Undoubtedly he was not paying attention and walked right into a small war party and found himself and the others surrounded. He recalls how the man next to him whispered they were dead men. Calmly they laid down their weapons and raised their arms above their heads. This allowed Malachi's shirt to lift above his waist revealing the signet. Immediately the man standing in the fringe of the clearing flashed anger then confusion as he pushed his way through the crowd to stand right in the face of Malachi. Up unto this point Malachi had never feared anything. This impressive man stood about two foot taller than himself. Malachi noticed that when he stepped up and spoke there seemed to be a reverence for this man. He reached out and took a hold of the signet. Malachi thought that since the man standing before him was distracted he could take this opportunity to draw his knife and try his luck but thought better because even if he was lucky to kill this one there were still six more and he did not want to die this day. The expression of the aggressor's face changed and he spoke to Malachi in perfect English. This surprised everyone and they looked at each other amazed that such a sophisticated man could be as brutal as this. With a gentle voice that automatically calmed the situation. The tone and mannerism of the stranger was familiar to Malachi when the man introduced himself as his uncle. They spent the next few days walking and talking one to the other and Malachi learned a lot about the Seminoles. A people he learned to respect and admire because they lived the life he had always longed for.

These renegades forced everyone living to the south and east of the fort to find refuge inside the fort. A regiment of volunteers was gathered and plans made for six days to head south along the main trail to Fort

Gatlin. The aim of this trip was to locate them and force them south to the Everglades. Captain Sullivan asked since Malachi had already traveled the route between the two forts on several occasions if he would be willing to lead the regiment on the safest course. They agreed on terms then Malachi stood making sure Captain Sullivan understood he was not enlisting and would staying only long enough it will take to complete task, shaking hand then turned and walked out the door. A cool breeze blew from the northwest hitting him right in the face. From the moment he stepped out onto the porch he was chilled to the bone. He wishes now he would have brought his jacket as he climbs a top his horse and presses his blunt spurs in the side of his horse.

Looking around he could see things had changed a lot since he was last here. The one thing that troubled him the most was the amount of new families now living here. He wanted to find a place that was not as crowded to start a family but was not sure if Mollie wanted same. Over the last few weeks he had thought a lot about asking Mollie to marry him because he remembered what her father had said while on the trip and it had gotten harder to keep his promise lately. This is another reason why he needed to get away for a while. He had talked to Captain Sullivan a few more times. Since he was an older man he sought his advice about marriage and life. The captain told him he was married once but it did not last long and that was the extent of his experience. After they spoke Malachi made up his mind that he would ask her. He promised when he got back from Fort Gatlin they would get married if she would wait.

That night after washing up in the small pond east of the camp Malachi asked if he could speak to Mollie's father. They walked out into the darkness down a well used path. He knew they needed not worry because the path they had chosen to camp on was a trail used by cows as they wondered free through this area. The glow of the lightered stick taken from the fire illuminated his face as he lit his pipe. Uncertain Malachi shuffled his feet unsure if this was truly what he wanted at this time when he at long last started to speak. Even though it was cooler than usual sweat poured from his fore head and a sick feeling invaded his stomach. He had never been this anxious even when he had Indians shooting at him. Mollie's father seeing his nervousness spoke up breaking the silence saying. "What do you want, Malachi? I ain't got all night." His insensitivity irritated Malachi when he just flat out asked if he could marry Mollie. Before he could answer Mollie dashed from the shadows almost knocking Malachi to the ground. Both men were surprised by the reality that Mollie had been listening to their conversation and before her father could chasten her Malachi spoke harshly to her, surprisingly causing her to cower behind a sheepish smile. Dropping her head she looks at her feet embarrassed as her father looked at Malachi and smiled telling him he will do. He turns and walks toward the fire glowing in the oak hammock that had been the temporary camp while they cleared and build the cabin. He left Malachi and Mollie standing in the darkness admonishing them they needed to wait until they were married. His warning embarrassed Malachi and he assured him they would not do anything that would bring shame to him. They stood there for a few moments before Mollie reached out touching Malachi on the arm sending waves of excitement through his body. He took her in his arms and kissed her as they fell to the ground.

The sun started to rise when Malachi woke up realizing he had broken his promise to Mollie's father and Mr. Blackburn. He felt ashamed along with an awkward calmness he could not explain, but not a guilty feeling. The whole night was blurry and cemented his commitment to Mollie. He woke her and was met with a devilish smile, she said. "Good morning. When do you plan to leave?" Malachi told her she needed to hurry back to camp so her father would not think anything happened. She said. "Silly, something did happen and us hiding it does not change that. But if you want me to I will do as you say. I love you Malachi. I cannot wait until you get back." Malachi smiled at her taking his hat in his hand, turns and walks into the brush. He must have walked a mile trying hard to remember what happened last night.

Nine months to the day the first cry of the two boys was born to Mollie and Malachi Tanner filled the small cracker style home on the high banks of the Econlockhatchee River. The eldest of their two was named Elijah Malachi Tanner. They called him "Lize". The baby was born not breathing and Aunt Penny worked feverishly to help him take his first breath. It was almost a miracle as the baby who had completely turned blue started to breath. Fourteen months later the youngest was born and he was named Henry Lee George Tanner, they called him "JT" for short.

Malachi had accomplished most of what he wanted to do by the time Lize turned fifteen. It was early December 1908 when Malachi began to run a high fever. There was nothing Mollie could do to break the fever and within three days Malachi slipped into a deep sleep. After that he only lasted another day. Just before he passed away he wakes and weakly tells Mollie he loved her dearly and he is so sorry he could not do anything else for her. Between labored breaths he called for the boys, first telling JT his mother and brother would need him now more than ever. JT could never remember his father showing such affection. Placing his hand under the covers he struggles to lift the large knife he had carried ever since he himself was a small boy asking JT to care for it and remember him. Next Lize climbed into the bed with his father and begged him not to leave as tears poured from his eyes. With that he slipped away from them. When Lize realized his beloved father was gone he went crazy with grief. Violently he destroys everything in sight, throwing one of the chairs through the newly installed screens. He would have ruined everything but JT was able to physically restrain him, dragging him out into the yard. Having his father's demeanor JT spoke to Lize and he began to claim down. He assured him their mother needed them to grow up and finish what their father started. Something happen to Lize that day, something JT did not understand but it was if Lize grew up right before his eyes. Automatically he became serious about everything. The next morning without being asked Lize picked up a shovel found a place not far from the front door of the meager home they shared with their mother and started digging a grave. JT watched from the shadows as he dug stopping ever so often while he cried bitterly begging for an answer to his question. Why? A tear rolls down JT's cheek. His sorrow was not because he lost his father but for Lize and his mother. He now was going to have to lead this family. A heavy load sets upon him and he asked for help to bear up and carry it without question. Later that evening all alone they loaded their father into the wagon and walked solemnly toward the single hole in the ground. Lize and JT lowered the man who had been the rock of their family into the cold ground and turned to their mother looking for some more direction. Neither of the boys had never done this before. She was only able to say a few words when she broke under the pressure and sorrow. This scared JT more than the loss of his father because he had never seen her react this way. He had always believed his mother the strongest of the family and if she was not able to bear this what would he do.

The last shovel full of dirt was thrown into the hole. The sun was beginning to set and the brightness and color of the glow was refreshing in a way. They headed back to the house. As soon as they entered the clearing they could hear their mother back in the kitchen singing her song again this helped JT to face the challenges of life without his father.

CHAPTER 9

After the death of Malachi Tanner, Mollie his beloved and devoted wife feared she would not be able to care for the boys. She kept the land Malachi had worked so hard to clear. Even though well equipped and enough supplies, how were they going to work the farm and cows. She would sit for hours after the twins were asleep praying to God if by chance God could send her daddy. She was confident in the fact her daddy would know what to do but she believed her faith to be too small. Every day the work got harder and the day shorter then way after dark she would collapse into bed. The boys did not demand much of her time. JT was independent and required little while Lize did not know he needed anything so the littlest thing would entertain him for hours.

Early one day after hitching the mule Mollie was preparing to plow when she heard the clanking of trace chains and a wagon bouncing down the lane. This sound was easily recognized but not often heard out so far from civilization. Her heart begins to beat faster the closer it drew to the house. She hurried to the boys as they slept soundly on the quilt she had laid next to the open field. She hid behind a palmetto patch when her eyes fixed on the mule as she moved to where she herself could see what was coming. The mule normally was not easily spooked but she wanted to get as far away from the noise as she could. Mollie fretted if she did not leave her hiding place soon the mule could possibly destroy the plow and she knew she did not have the money to replace it. Grabbing the edge of the quilt she pulled the boys closer to covering. Turning she watches for a few more seconds hoping to move at the right moment allowing enough time to unhook the mule then get back to the boys. She was well in the open when she heard a man's voice call saying. "Howdy. Dis da Tanner's place?" Mollie freezes. Her mind tries to figure out what she should do. Should she run in the opposite direction drawing the intruder away from her babies? No. This would not be a wise choice because if she was caught then her children would be left to fend for themselves. What should she do?

She turns racing back to where she had left the boys. Half way there her feet got tangled in some grapevines causing her to trip hitting the ground. Her breath was knocked from her but she manages to roll on her back. She knew this was it as she crawled wildly toward the boys begging this stranger to leave them alone.

Behind her she hears heavy footsteps when all of a sudden she feels two hands grab her shoulder calling her name. She collapse and starts to cry uncontrollably when Mollie heard the calming voice of her mother. Sally drops down to her knees pulling her to her breast rubbing her hair trying to calm her. After taking a deep breath Mollie looks into her eyes finally recognizing her. By now the boys were a wake and crying. Two small girls raced past Mollie like a flash gathering the boys trying to quiet the boys.

Mollie finally calmed down and she was able to talk to her mother. Her first question was the whereabouts of her father and who was the stranger she was riding with. Sally sat down and began to cry. She told her he was killed by a tree falling on him about three months earlier. She was as she is now all alone. Mr. Penny-money lived on the farm next to theirs and he was a widower with twin girls. Sally drew Mollie close to her taking her by the hand. Taking a deep breath she continued by telling the arrangement was mutual because both needed help.

As the boys grew Mollie could tell Lize was not as sharp as JT. She feared the lack of breathing when he was born caused his problem but she was not completely sure. While in Kissimmee they visited the new doctor confirming her suspicions and he told to let him do what he could. They grew much taller than their father. Their childhood was difficult but Mollie did her best to raise them to be the men they would soon become.

CHAPTER 10

JT awakes to the sound of heavy dew as it drops like rain from the towering cabbage trees on a small island south of Lake Monroe. With each drop of dew the hissing of the fire being put out was only a reminder of the days coming task. He not sure but he believes today is his thirtieth birthday. He stretches kicking aside the mosquito net. Grabbing for his boots he almost forgets to dump them out because he really had to pee. Shaking his left boot out rolled a small pigmy rattlesnake. The small snake was just as surprised as JT was when it rolled out next to the fire. Without thinking JT reached for the stick coved with the black soot of the lightered fire used to lift his coffee pot bring it down on his head. The snake twisted into a small ball ending up on its back. The commotion demanded the attention of the dogs. Their curiosity got the best of them they just had to investigate. JT hollered. "No!" All the dogs but one stubborn half cur and bulldog had to stick his nose down to get just one sniff. JT using the same stick used to kill the rattlesnake reached out just touched the dog in the rear end. You should have seen the dog jump. He cleared the fire and hollered like something had a hold of him. His legs never stopped moving until he hit the ground finally getting traction. When he thought he was at a safe distance he turned growled every hair bristled on his back. JT laughed out loud when he remembered he needed to pee. Slipping on his other boot standing he stretched again. That pain in his back still affected his ability to get going first thing of a morning. Limping off to the edge of the camp he peed and wouldn't you know it that stupid dog was right there watching. Before JT could finish his business that dump dog hiked his leg and started to pee on his leg when he crossed the line. JT kicked the need to pee right out of that dog. A sharp pain caused him to fall to the ground. He had not felt this pain before. It took his breath, reaching for a small cedar sapling than used it to help lift his self to a standing position. When finally he got to his feet waves of nausea hit him. He dry heaved and it echoed throughout the small island. He staggered to the edge of the water. Falling to his knees, with great effort he lifted the cool tannic water washing his face. He stayed on his knees for several minutes not by choice but necessity drinking more than a few sips of water. At long last the feeling of sickness left but the experience left him drained. Managing to stagger to his feet he stand for a few minutes to help alleviate the pain and dizziness then stumbles back to his camp dropping to his knees. He fumbled around in his wallet taking out a few pieces of dried venison and chewing savoring the juices. He could feel his strength return and in the right position he could feel the pain subside.

The lowing of the cows caught his attention. He could not stay here much longer or it will be too hot to do anything. It took about five minutes for him to gather all his stuff and pack it away in his wallet. Using the last of the coffee to douse the fire white steam rose and was quickly dissipated by a hard breeze from the southwest. This is first moment JT became aware of the strong breeze. For this time of year a breeze like this meant rain.

After saddling his horse and securing his bedroll and wallet to his saddle he rode as quickly as he could out onto the marsh. The southern sky was dark. You could actual see the thunder clouds roll and churn. Dark gray encircled but lighter gray clouds. A tinge of red intermixed. JT recalls the old saying. "Red skies in the morning sailor take warning, red skies at night sailor's delight." Unrolling his sixteen foot cow wipe he called for the dogs to gather the cows finishing his command with a loud echoing crack. The dogs darted toward the cows like torpedoes in the needle grass.

All his gear was sopping wet including his extra shirt. Yesterday he suffered from being shafted and was miserable all afternoon. He hoped to have dry clothes but the rain saw fit to this not happening. The days are beginning to get really hot. The dogs spend a lot of time trying to stay cool in the swift running water of the St. Johns River. Just last week he lost one of his best dogs to a big gator. All he could do was to watch helplessly as the old dog swam franticly toward the shore when all of a sudden the water erupted only to be pulled under never to be seen again. JT knew he needed to get the cows and dogs away from the water's edge but knew as well if he were to turn east the scrub gets thick and there is little water.

Plus he is on a schedule only a few more days and he will meet up with the main herd.

This bunch of cows was particularly fussy and hard to keep bunched. If it were not for the dogs he would have abandon them and come back with some help. He liked watching the dogs work the cows. First thing in the morning an old brindled cow with sharp horns decided she did not want to stay with the lot. She broke and run. The dogs were right on her heels nipping her until she finally stopped to fight. The little cur mixed ring neck dog jumped grabbing her by the nose rolling tossing her to the ground. She bellowed loudly regained her footing throwing the little dog high into the air. When he landed, he was right back attached to her nose. He aggravated her until she could only find peace back in the bunch. She stood defiantly shaking her head. The long horns spanning about four feet across almost caused her to stumble but she stared rebelliously as JT passed. He laughed at her then called for the dogs to get them started. Slowly at first then in a single file line as they passed through a thick willow pond. JT realized one of his dogs was missing. He whistled and the dogs circled the cows forcing them to stop. This delay aggravated JT. Way off to the east he could hear the dog baying. Standing an top of the saddle so he could see over the tall palmettos bordering the pond he could see it opened up and it would be easier going. So he whistled again forcing the cows to move in that direction. It was really thick but he allowed the cows to pick their own way after all they broke through. JT stopped, coursed the baying dog and headed in that direction. He had not gone far when he caught a strong odor of bore hog. He immediately knew what the dog had done. He had jumped a hog and had him stopped.

The other dogs left the cows and joined the baying. JT rode up the high blue looking palmetto patch. Tied his horse and slipped into the palmettos carrying a small long rope. He cut a pole. Wrapped it around the end and eased it through the fronds. He maneuvered it around the long tusk pulled and the instance the rope tightened the dogs caught him by both ears. The fight was on and it took JT several minutes to get him on his side and tied. They are too far from home so he decided to cut him and mark him with his mark. The work was quick as he cut the last of the crop split in the right ear. His next thought was to cut off his tail like Little John Nettles always did but this practice annoyed him so he would not do that to the next person to catch him. Still sitting on the hog he surveyed his surrounding deciding on his way of escape. Taking a deep breath he jumped from off his back. He kicked violently trying to right himself. His whole purpose was to afflict as much harm to JT as he hurt him. But JT was too fast and the dogs made sure the hog would not follow. He reached the horse and in a single movement jumped on his back and was clear of the palmetto patch. He whistled and the dog returned to get the cow moving again.

After sitting in the saddle for several hours the pain JT woke with had become almost unbearable. He must have sleep wrong or something but he knew if he ever got down he would catch heck trying to get back in. The longer he rode the black it become. The first blistering drops of rain hit him just as he saw Pine Island in the distance. Only about a mile from his destination he whistled to the dogs. This particular whistle brought the dogs to a keener attention and they began to work closer as a team. JT was always amazed at how smart a dog was. He untied and unfurled his whip swinging it making it pop loud echoing off the cabbage trees bordering the sandy lane leading toward the pens.

The crack of the whip caught the attention of Wash who had gotten to Pine Island about noon with his bunch of cows. Reluctantly he left the front porch of the small cabin on the edge of the clearing. His presence startled JT causing him to flinch and the pain become more intense. Wash raced across the clearing when the bottom fell out. The rain fell so hard and so heavy the cow pens disappeared. In seconds both men were drenched. The rain made it difficult to keep the cows bunched but the dogs never let up and finally the last stubborn cow trotted through the gate. With a word JT rode toward the small lean-to slipped from the saddle unhitched the girth allowing the saddle to drop beside the horse. Wash had scooped a scoop of whole corn from JT wallet. Poured it into the wooden trough and the horse ate hungrily. The look of pain on JT's face told Wash his best friend was in pain. He grabbed his gear and walked beside him to the front porch. JT managed to get his boots of. Taking off his wet clothes which usually brought some sarcastic remark fro Wash but today that was absent. Wash had cooked a pot of venison stew along with the warmth of the fire in the wood burning stove helped JT to relax. After eating and taking a long swig of Wash's medicine, really called moon-shine he laid down next to the fore and fell into a deep sleep and dreams of how it use to be.

1900

Three years later JT found his mother dead at the wash shed. Unsure of how long she had been there before he discovered her. He called for Lize who was in the freshly plowed garden plot and told him of what he had discovered. His only reaction was to head to the barn and disappear in the direction of his father's grave carrying the shovel over his left shoulder. JT was relieved his brother did not react to the news of their mother's death like he did their father's. Lize had grown much stronger than JT and he was unsure if he could physically control him as he did that day.

Lize and JT stood next to another pile of dirt marking the grave of their dearly loved mother. Her death seemed to be easier for JT than that of his father. He figured this enemy now so familiar to him having to help bury his father, grandparents, uncles, aunts and the baby lost several months after his father passed away standing at this spot was nothing new. He truly missed his mother because it was from her he drew his strength.

Lize wanted to stick close to their childhood home but JT had a need to wonder. Knowing he could not leave Lize alone. The older Lize got the more confused he had become and was now totally dependent upon JT. He could not even go to the outhouse without Lize wanting to know what he is doing. This annoyed JT but with patience he accepted this responsibility.

CHAPTER 11

The sun had been up for about two hours. The cool of the morning quickly vanished as its rays streaked through the towering cabbage trees. The smoke from a lightered knot fire in the midst of the cow camp swirled around causing a smoky haze to form under the canopy of cabbage fans then upward disappearing in the slight western breeze. The clanking of a coffeepot and cast iron dutch-oven is soon replaced by the whinnying of horses and the creaking of leather as the cow hunters saddle their horses. The muffled sound of private conversations could be heard between the screech of the coot as it howlers flapping its wings while running from one bank of the river to the other. In the distance one could hear the lowing of a cow as she calls for her calf that had been separated from her as they try to wean them.

Off to one side of the camp JT in his wide brim high crown brown felt hat throws his saddle a top a small red roan horse. With methodical and thoughtless exertion he reached under the horse and cinched it tightening it for the day's activity. JT stood about five foot eleven inches tall. Wearing a dingy white long sleeve shirt with his washed out grayish blue britches that are tucked in to his knee high lace up leather boots. Thin as a rail he towers over the small horse as he places his left foot in the stirrup, hops once right up into the saddle then adjust his self in the saddle knowing this will be his station for the rest of the day. JT had always been teased about how his feet looks like the almost drag the ground, if you were close to him as he passed through palmettos you would hear him cuss a little about his feet getting drug out of the stirrup.

Lize was almost a foot taller than JT. He wore britches dyed dark blue which could be mistaken for black, brogan boots and a dull white long sleeve with garters up on his arm. He wore a small brim light colored hat pulled down covering his sickly eyes. He did not speak much until he and JT were alone because JT was the only one that did not ask him to repeat himself. When Lize began to talk JT could not get a word in edge wise. The horse he rode was slick black with what some would call a blaze down his face. He was not as sure footed as the smaller more rugged horses the other rode but if ever he got his rope on a bad cow it was definitely going somewhere. His slicker and bed roll draped disorganized behind his saddle covering the flank area of the horse. He leads his horse toward the fire taking care to kick enough dirt onto the fire to extinguish it. Satisfied it was safe to leave he grabbed the horn and the back of the saddle and in one fluid motion rose up and found an uncomfortable seat back in the saddle. He joked saying he would probably die in the saddle so he might as well get use to it.

The last of the riders was called Wash, short for Washington Micah Crawford emerged from the palmetto patch behind the camp re-buckling his stained off white britches, faded red shirt that be had purchased in Kissimmee the year before for his uncle's wedding. He was only a few inches taller than JT and rode an old yellow nag of a horse. She was not much to look at but JT was jealous of her stamina and understanding of a cow. It took little effort for him to pop up and into the saddle. The three men now stare out onto the open span of the St. Johns River marsh reminding each other again how much they each loved the river. From the smell of a lightered fire mixed with the aroma of the marsh to the gentle sound of the flowing of the tannic water. The flight of birds as the passed over head was a sign of the perfectness of the day. There seems to be something unspoken and magical about a sun rise and sun set while camping and cow hunting on the St. Johns River was almost breath-taking.

Remembering in what direction they last heard the cow lowing than stepping from the protection of the thick cabbage hammock into the cold breeze as it cuts through their light jackets. JT hoped that the day would not turn out to be a hot one. In Central Florida you could freeze in the morning and burn up in the afternoon only to have to huddle next to a blazing fire at dark.

Under Wash's feet trotted four head of dogs. All of the dogs were extremely excited and apt to take off after a hog if they happened across one.. Wash used his bull whip to keep them from running ahead and spooking the cows. All the dogs knew better than to get out of line because the sixteen foot whip could unfurled at the speed of lightening and cause great harm. A little ring necked yellow dog learned this all too well when he figured he would do what he wanted then experienced the pain of disobedience.

Their plan was to head straight for "Josh's Hole". This is a very deep hole on the St. Johns River where anytime of the year whether it is dry or flooded you can catch catfish. No one really knows why it was named "Josh's Hole" but it really did not matter to them so they never asked the reason. JT loved to fish and this was his favorite place.

They then turned due west and rode through a thick cabbage hammock having towering cedar trees. In places where the cold could not touch directly the dog fennels were so thick the riders often lost sight of each other. The reason for coming this way was to visit with old man Streetman. The Streetman's lived about half the year in a small two room log cabin opposite of Possum Hammock on the cedar ridge across the river. It was unusually built cabin with a low roof in order to keep the house cool in the hot and humid summer. JT wanted to ask if he, while out and about had seen any cows bearing their mark.

The river was slowly changing because of the dredging down south. The once well defined course of the river was sufficient for the steamers from the north to carry supplies to the pioneers of this area now have difficulty and have been forced to stop at Lake Cane just south of Orange Mound. For years the deep and shallow running boats brought supplies to Lake Cane. A road was constructed coming from Christmas was well used but now the river was becoming too shallow for them to navigate the river. For thousands of years the river marsh has flooded naturally cutting its way through the lowest areas. But now with the water being diverted away from its natural flow the lush green grasses suffered because of the lack of water or too much of it. This is a great concern for the cowmen who depend on the river marsh to feed the large herds they had accumulated over the years. Once massive herds could be seen on the river marsh along with large herds of horses but now just a few find enough here. (Recently several of the local cowmen had been noticing some sick cows and have alerted their neighbors to be on the watch. This is the main reason why JT, Lize and Wash were riding the river marsh.)

Mr. Streetman heard the three riders coming long before they actually got close. Wash had to use his whip a lot since entering the long hammock running all the way to Jim Creek. The hogs used this hammock this time of year filling the bellies with the cabbage berries that fall. The ones they were able to see were in good shape but the left them standing because their mission was more important. The old man shaken comes and meets them at the edge of the clearing. They could tell something was wrong. JT had met Mr. Streetman on several occasions and never knew him to be excitable but that morning was different. He warned them that two of his children were bad sick with the fever and needed a doctor. The closest one is in Kissimmee. He told them he could not leave because he feared the worst would happen and he wanted to stay close for the rest of his family. He had commented about the unusually large number of ticks this year and how they had to dig several from behind the girl's ears. He spoke to JT telling him he was going to gather some of his nearest neighbors and try to burn as soon as he could. The practice of burning was tow fold, first to produce a good growth of wire and other natural growing grasses on the scrub and to kill the ticks.

JT spoke up and voluntaries to ride straight for the Simmons place who lived on Cox Creek and bring Aunt Penny. He assured Mr. Streetman he would not stop until he brought them back promising he would return as fast as possible with Aunt Penny. She was the local mid-wife and able to help anyone recover from any sickness. Just before he turned Mr. Streetman reached out taking JT firmly with his large hand squeezing hard and without saying a word JT knew the urgency.

Early the next morning just as the sun began to send its orange-red streaks across the eastern horizon. A low fog hangs suspended just above the palmetto flats JT rode up into the Simmons clearing. A single light burns inside the old cracker style house. Just as he was about to call out to anyone in the house he became startled by the soft voice of an old lady just behind him. JT was breathing hard making him to hesitate in answering when Aunt Penny pushed past JT and onto the front porch. She said in passing, "When you can member what ya want, I'll be inside. It's awful cold out here fer an old woman." Her firmness brought JT around and as she reached the top step he said. "Mr. Streetman sent me fer ya. Two of his youngens' is bad sick and he needs ya bad." She stops and begins to ask him a series of question that he could not answer. He told her that as soon as he got to the Streetman's he left and headed here. He told her that he had been riding since mid yesterday morning. Aunt Penny invited JT in for a hot cup of coffee and some biscuits and guava jelly. He ate feverishly knowing they would probably be leaving soon. Aunt Penny woke up her two oldest children barking orders for them to gather the needed herbs.

Pa Simmons headed to the barn and hooked up the ox to the cart. As the children returned handing their bundle to their ma Aunt Penny climbed into the cart settling down behind her husband who will go a long on this trip because it had been a long time since the last time he was able to visit with the Streetman's.

JT wanted to ride ahead but he enjoyed talking to the old man and old woman. He was amazed by their homespun wisdom and watched carefully as she stop along the way and gathered other herbs for the treating of the common sicknesses and others just in case it is worst than what she figured. They only stopped when either of them needed to relieve themselves and ate what Aunt Penny had packed for the trip. About a mile away they stopped and Aunt Penny told JT to go a kill her a fresh piece of meat so she could make a broth for the sick children. He turned and disappeared into the cedar hammock along the trail. He had not traveled long before he began to see good sign on a well used trail. Dismounting JT tied his horse to a small myrtle bush pulling his single shot rifle from its sheath. He eased along the trail with the wind in his face. The sun was quickly setting when movement caught his attention. Straining his vision against the dimming of the day he was able to make out the form of a small doe as she fed unaware of his presence. He positioned himself in an open lane the deer was making her way to when he took aim. Squeezing the trigger the small animal fell in her tracks. He stood for a few seconds watching the brown form for any movement. Satisfied the deer was dead JT walked up, slitting its throat and gutting and dragging her to his horse. Replacing the rifle in his sheath then hoisting the doe to the saddle in front of him he makes hast toward the Streetman's.

When JT rode up in the clearing Wash walked up followed by Lize. Wash asked Lize if he would take the deer from JT because he wanted to talk to him. Without a word Lize carried the deer to the butchering table and without thinking skinned the deer and carried it to Mrs. Streetman. Wash whispered that the reason for the girl's sickness was ticks on the back of her neck. It didn't take long for Aunt Penny to find the ticks but it will take the girls a long time to over it.

The three young men spent the night waiting for news about the little girl fighting the last of the mosquitoes. Just before they retired for the night Mr. Streetman came to their fire and sat down. He just stared into the fire becoming almost hypnotized by the dancing of the flames. His eyes were red from crying. JT looked at Wash then to Lize confused by the presence of the man just sitting without saying a word. Wash reached for the smutty coffee pot sitting next to the fire and poured a steaming hot cup of black coffee handing it to Mr. Streetman. The smell brought him out of his daze. He finally spoke to JT apologizing to him for his brief absence and asked if any of them had steady work. This question brought all the young men to attention. JT asked him what he meant. The old man took a long gulp of coffee commenting on how satisfying coffee was while sitting next to a good fire. Everyone agreed and pressed him for information about the work he was referring to. They had grown tired of drifting and fishing. For the past three weeks they had fished and sold the fish they had caught to a fish house in Sanford. They would sell their fish to a buyer who would come to Lake Cane on a weekly basis. They enjoyed fishing but Wash said you can get too much of a good thing and he was tired of it. Mr. Streetman cleared his throat and told JT.

"I knowed yer pa. He was a good man. So I'm goen' to hep ya. Do ya know where Will Magrit's place is? He has fermation bout the state needen riders. Go to see him and he will hep ya."

JT stood extending his right hand to the old man and thanked him for the fermation and assured him they would head there first thing in the morning.

JT, Wash and Lize were in the saddle way before daylight. Their hope was to make it to the Magrit place before noon. They did not want to miss out on this job opportunity. Times were getting hard with the disappearing of the smaller cowmen. When there were more herds owned by different cowmen there seemed to be a lot more work.

They finally emerged from the cabbage and cedar hammock bordering the St. Johns River Marsh. They thought of stopping by and seeing if anyone were home at the Boar's Nest but decided against it because it took longer to cross Jim Creek Swamp then they thought. It had rained and Poka-taw Flats was flooded making it difficult crossing it until Wash remembered a high ridge running from the head waters of Tosohatchee Creek to the Econlockhatchee River. Even though they will come out of the flats five miles north of the Magrit place but it will be easier to make their way south along the creek swamp. The sun was beginning to fade behind the tree line of the Econlockhatchee River. Lize had complained about being chaffed ever since they crossed Jim Creek so to get a little peace JT decided to stop for the night. As soon as the horses were taken care of and secured Lize undressed and without any shame walked around camp naked as a jay bird. JT finally told him to sit down because he was tired of looking at his butt. Lize stood in the light of the fire shaking his bottom toward JT when he picked up a stock from a burnt cabbage fan and stuck it toward him when Lize squealed and cussed at JT. JT never touched him with it but by the way he complained you would have thought he was burnt to the bone. JT nor Wash ever considered mosquitoes as a blessing until this night. They were so bad Lize could not stand them eating every inch of his naked body so he relented and even before they were dry Lize put his clothes back on. JT told him he was glad he learned his lesson. JT could not sleep for listening to Lize snore. He was glad Lize's snoring couldn't be used as a Malachiing call because he would have every hog, bear and panther for miles. Finally about three o'clock JT drifted off to sleep. He would receive his best rest during this time and would awake renewed and ready for a day of hard work.

Wash was gone the next morning when JT finally woke. This was not unusual for Wash, he was a wonderer and JT had often thought he would not be able to settle down and one day just vanished. About an hour later Wash rode back into camp. He was carrying a jug tied to the horn of his saddle singing to the top of his lungs and sounds like someone had a rooster by the neck. At first JT thought Indians were torturing him or he had caught a wildcat and was beating it with a lightered knot. His singing woke Lize up and when he took his first step immediately he believed he was hurting. The chaffing from the day before caused him in a lot of pain. Before anyone could say anything Lize had stripped naked again and stood next to the fire fanning himself. Wash told Lize he knew how to fix it but he had to look at it first. Lize reluctantly agreed JT looked confused as to why Wash would want to get that close to Lize without any clothes on. As Wash stepped forward and took a big swig from the jug. Everyone thought he swallowed it but he hadn't. When he bent forward to get close enough he spit a mouthful of moon shine on the raw places between his legs setting Lize afire. He did not burn his butt literally but the effects of the moon shine on the open blisters set him on fire. You should have seen him jumping around bucking like a green broke mare with an inexperienced rider. He hooped and hollered for about an hour. Lize did not know his own strength so Wash had to do some fast talking to keep Lize from really hurting him. It did cost Wash something and that was the rest of the shine he had in his jug. Lize smashed it and laughed about the look on Wash's face when he realized he had no more shine. They spend another night so Lize could recover. JT was uneasy and wanted to leave this place but knew they would experience further delay if Lize got infected. What was meant for a joke turned out to be a good cure and Lize was ready to ride the next morning.

They rode in single file line through the thick, head high palmettos. JT took lead. The only time any were able to ride side by side was when they came to an open pond where the palmettos were not as high as on the scrub. Off in the distance they could see an orange grove and each knew they were not far from the Magrit place. The conversation relaxed as they entered the large improved pasture. Off in the distance they could see herds of deer feeding. Lize wanted to go ahead and kill one for their supper but JT did not believe that to be a good idea being so close to the house. He did not think Mr. Magrit would appreciate that at all.

Opening the gate they continued up the sandy trail leading to the old house on the Econlockhatchee River. The closer they got the louder the dogs barked alerting anyone for miles around of their presence. Lize had his dogs on ropes to keep them from rushing forward to meet the other dogs to fight. He had one old jip that would fight anything at anytime. She thought she was bad but got whipped ever time. He unrolled his whip and used it once quickly calming his dogs. As they rounded the last palmetto patch there standing on the front porch was a man that neither, Wash and Lize had ever met before. JT met him only once while working cows for the Yates south of Kissimmee. He was unsure if he would remember him. Before they were able to stop Will Magrit called JT by name; which immediately relaxed the young men. JT greeted him back as the others simply nodded their head awkwardly acknowledging him. He climbed down from atop his horse and shares with him their reason for coming and seeing him uninvited. Mr. Magrit invited them to get down and sit a while of which they did. After talking for several hours about anything that came up Will invited them to stay the night and they would talk about the new work tomorrow.

CHAPTER 12

About an hour before daylight the dogs stirred waking JT. The moon was still about full and the dull light flooded the oak hammock. He rubbed the sleep from his eyes, stretched, straining to make out the form as it moved from the front porch toward the barn. Their camp was situated on the east side of the house under some scrub oak trees. The foul stench of rotting guavas filled the air. JT sits up, reaches for his boots pulling them on than makes his way across the opening toward the barn that now stood open. In the rear he could hear someone milling around washed in the faint glow of a oil lamp. J'T' called out, his voice echoed. He was quickly answered by the stern voice of Will Magrit. "I'm here, back of the barn."

JT made his way around the cluttered barn finding Mr. Magrit with his head stuck in the corn crib. He straightened up holding several dried corn cobs in his hand handing them to JT and said. "Make yer self useful, I got to feed up fore I put you'll to work." JT looked surprised at what Mr. Magrit said. "Put ya to work."

He was hoping for work but was stunned they were going to start this soon. JT helped him rub corn from the cobs as they spoke. Mr. Magrit told him he had six hundred acres needing fencing. The subject of fencing had always been taboo and something that was avoided because of the open range, a sure fire way of causing trouble with neighbors and those who still hunted for cows. JT respectfully questioned Mr. Magrit as to why he was going ahead with something that could potently cause him trouble. To which he was quickly answered with irritation. "Texas Tick Fever, it could kill ever cow I got." JT had heard of the Texas Tick but did not believe it was a real threat. Mr. Magrit assured him it was real and restated he was trying to protect his cows.

The sun had risen and light washed the clearing. They watched with amusement as the other two young men began to stir around the fire. Mr. Magrit hesitated and told JT they would be paid twelve dollars a week until the job was done, he did not care how long it took as long as it was done right. He went on to say that Uncle Bunyan and several others were out on the flats cutting cypress post. "You'll bein by hepen' them. I figured we'd need bout six thousand post to start with. Lize is your younger or older brother?" JT looked puzzled by the question when he responded. "We're twins. He ani't that smart but he's a good worker." "Good," said the old man as he steps from the front porch, stuffing a chew of tobacco into his mouth. "He'll be with Bunyan cutten lightered post for the corners. You need to make sure he's awake and feed him good, they'll be here soon to get him. I got some axes in the barn and be careful they're sharp." He then turned and headed toward the hog pen to feed the hogs as JT turned and headed toward where they were camping.

JT hollered for Wash to get up and for Lize to hurry and get dressed because Mr. Magrit had hired them for twelve dollars a week. Wash jumped to his feed and commented how he had never seen twelve dollars much less had twelve dollars in his pocket at one time. They were excited about the chance of working and asked what they would be doing. As JT sat down and put the coffee pot back on the fire he told them they would be cutting post to build fence around six hundred acres. Before JT could finish his sentence Wash exploded telling him he did not want anything to do with crusaded fences and he would not be a part of it. When Mr. Magrit spoke up and said then there ani't no work here for you. His presence surprised even JT for he had not notice the tall old man standing at the edge of the camp. Wash was hot tempered and started gathering his gear when Mr. Magrit spoke again. "There ani't no work for anyone these days, most of the land now belongs to the timber companies. You may can find work at the turpentine camps south of here or you can head north and cut cross ties for a dollar a day. It's up to you."

Wash spoke up and said, "no disrespect but there's people who'll kill over fences. I heared of a crew getten shot up round Jacksonville, I ain't wantten to go looken for trouble." Mr. Magrit standing tall and resolute said. "They'll be no trouble here. This is my place and I am protecting what's mine,"

"Protecting from what?" asked Wash as he made his way toward Mr. Magrit in a non-threatening way. "Texas Tick Fever" he spoke in kind of an irritated tone. "I've already lost forty cows and calves and I don't intend on losing any more." In a child like manner Lize asked. "Texas Tick Fever, what's that? It is a tick that's made its way from Texas. It's destroying whole herds, if we don't get a handle on it now it'll put me and a lot of families out of the business." The three young men looked perplexed by his statement.

As they were looking at each other bewildered, Uncle Bunyan and several men drove up in front of the house in a Model-t Runabout Roadster and got out. Because of Bunyan's size the dusty car rocked back and forth as he set to the ground looking strangely at the three strangers and he walked up to Will and shook his hand. Will introduced JT and his companions and told Henry Lee that Lize would be going to help him cut lightered post and the others will help with cutting the cypress post out on the flats. Lightered was the heart of the tall pine. Some trees stood fifty feet high and the wood so hard one could even chip a good ax. It was used for many things including kindling to start fires.

JT had never worked so hard in his life but what made it more difficult was the constant complaining of Wash. JT enjoyed the work and had gotten to where he could cut three hundred post himself a day. The cypress pond was full of water and after just a few days he learned not to allow the post to set in the water this made them heavier. Wash would continuously remind JT that he was not a logger but a cow hunter. To which Henry Lee finally got tired of his whining when he told him to go see Will and pick up his pay, he wasn't needed any more. He told him there were men looking for work and would like a chance to make the money he was making. Wash tried to talk Henry Lee into allowing him to continue but he had gotten a belly full of it, turned and returned to work. He had to walk back to the MaGrit place about ten miles away. Wash was still at the camp when JT returned about dark. Even though he was dog tired and wanted to go right to bed he sat up and listened to Wash late in the night. Wash told him he had heard they were hiring Ranger up in north Florida and that was what he was planning on doing as soon as he got his last bit of pay.

A Ranger Rider had a dual responsibility. First they were to ride and kill all the deer and any wild cow unmarked they happened upon. The reason for this was because they could not herd wild game carrying the tick. His other duty was to be present when the cattlemen dipped their cows making sure they dipped all of them. Each week the color dotted on the back of the cow as they left the vat changed. This was to keep dishonest cowmen from cheating. If the cowmen refused to dip his cows the Ranger was to shot the cows and not allow them to be turned out. JT was alarmed at news he was hearing from Wash and thought to himself this could be dangerous. There were law-abiding men who will refuse to change what they had done for years and allow a stranger to dictate to them what they had to door lose it all. JT knew this could start a war and a lot of good men will die. After talking to Wash, JT found Mr. Johnson and asked him about it. He affirmed Wash's story but was not sure they had begun hiring Ranger Riders as of yet. He went on to say if and when this happened he himself was going to sign on. But he warned JT it was going to be a messy job. He told of some trouble up in Clay County because they had already started dipping voluntary and thirteen vats were dynamited and three men had been killed trying to enforce dipping. Taking a long sip from the steaming cup of coffee he went on to tell of another west of them who was wrapped in barbed wire and tied to a tree. If it had not been for Indians he would have died out there on the scrub. This news scared JT and he awakens Wash and warns him but he would not listen.

At daylight the next morning Wash said his final good-byes and rode toward Kissimmee in hopes of hooking up with an outfit heading north. That was the last JT ever heard of Washington Micah Crawford.

CHAPTER 13

By nineteen hundred and six the Texas Tick had become a problem for the Florida cowmen. Many believe this infestation was due to all the cows that were being brought in from other states to replenish those lost to export. This was one of the main reasons why the Florida Cracker Cowman was leery of any new comer to the area and many of the new comers found it hard to be accepted especially those who tried to push their will upon them. The struggling cowmen did not like the idea of having to share what little pasture was left because this was their only livelihood and all they knew. They were raising large families and even though they did not intentionally plan for the future, the future of what they loved dearly was being threatened.

The hearty scrub cow seemed to be immune to the pest native to Florida. The mosquito that infected many cowmen and caused many to die because of malaria and other ailments did not affect the cow with the same sickness. Many cattlemen from out west found the native lush grasses of Florida's marshes and scrubs suited for sustaining many cattle and brought vast herds in. They found it was not as expensive to fatten cattle here as it was in Texas, Colorado and Montana and seeing Florida was surrounded by water the cows could be quickly shipped. There was a lot of money to be made and those who sought that wealth did not care for the dumb uneducated Florida Cracker, they soon learned different. There had a onetime been a good market and the possibility of shipping their fattened cattle north was expanding. Land was cheap here as well so whole ranches relocated.

It wasn't until this era of Florida and the cattle industry that the whip slowly became replaced by the stiff rope. It wasn't until they started bringing in new breeds to up-grade the stock that the problem for the self-reliant cowman became critical.

Many of the cowmen were visionaries so they began to fence their land long before fencing became mandatory in nineteen hundred and twenty three. It was during this year the state mandated the cattle dipping program. During this time as well the smaller cattlemen began to fight against the state and the idea of forcing them to put out the expense of dipping their cattle every fourteen days. Not only did they fight against the state but they found themselves in a battle for survival against their closest friend and even relatives. Many family disputes today can be traced back to this era in time. Brothers who once spent time together and raised their families within only a few miles of each other were forced to separate to survive.

Some had not been as fortunate enough to acquire large tracks of land so they depended upon the free range along the St. Johns River Marsh and the flat woods of central Florida. While others had large tracks of land had to sell in order to maintain during this hard time. Understand this this was not only a local problem but a dilemma; which crossed the entire state.

The Tick Fever had gotten so bad the State of Georgia constructed two fences along the border of the state restricting any Florida cattle to cross the state line. The Ranger Rider will be present when the cowmen herded their cattle to anyone of the thirty two hundred dipping vats constructed across the state. Every cow, calf, horse, mule, goat and sheep had to be dipped every fourteen days and any fur bearing animal had to be shot. This is one of the reasons why we do not see the vast herds of deer, wild horses and cow as we once had.

I am reminded of a story I heard about a man who owned a goat which ran with his herd that insisted on joining his comrades in jumping head long into the slurry of arsenic and water solution for his turn at being dipped. He would not be denied.

Herein lies the difficulty, for almost one hundred years pioneers turned cowmen moved in the open scrubs and along the river marshes of Florida and found a good but difficult living in the cows running free. It did not matter if they had one cow or one thousand cows everyone was considered a cowman. If that man had a resolute will and developed skill needed he could simply catch the illusive scrub cow that had evolved from the cows left by the Spaniards in the fifteen hundreds. Put their mark on the cow and raise a herd. Their cows in both large and small punches would roam free never having a need for fences or owning the land they used. Neighbor would help neighbor and no one would even think of stealing from or defrauding each other. But as more men moved in and began to purchase the land that had been freely used unhindered and as the once un-diminishable supply of cows dried up, men who were once friends and committed to each other's welfare now found themselves at odds.

Chapter 14

After the last post was packed and the final staple driven JT and Lize saddled their horse and followed Henry Lee and others out into the big scrub. Their task today and for as long as it took to gather all of the Magrit cows and those belonging to Henry Lee Tanner that had made their way from Big Prairie north east of Lake Cane. Will, JT, Lize and his dogs once they were out in the open scrub turned due south and rode toward Wewahootee. It had been several months since Will had visited and heard a strange whistle and wanted to see if rumors were true. He had heard they had run tracks for a rail road and built a hotel next to the community cow pens along the old road. This road led to Yeliehaw then further east toward the river and Cocoa.

Their first destination was to hunt the area around Settlement Slough where they found about thirty head of Magrit cows and twenty head of the Roberts cow from near Gridersville, driving the cows through the thick palmettos to the nearest set of pens that had been used for years. Here they separated the Roberts cows allowing them to wonder back into the open scrub. As soon as the gate was open they bolted, disappearing into the cut out pine flat. Will commented as they watched the last of the cows moved out of sight. Telling JT this area use to have pines towering seventy to eighty feet tall, the timber companies have destroyed the landscape. Scaring it with their deep rutted trail made by the large ox carts used to haul the timber to the rail road. Creeks that once held water all year long are dried up and when the rains come they become flooded and are impassable. He shakes his head with a disgusted look on his face then turns and rides away.

Leaving the cows securely shut up in the pens they turned and headed further east. Crossing Jim's Creek they entered the cabbage and cedar hammocks along the river marsh. The tall cabbages were blooming and the hammock was filled with the hum of bees as they worked the sweet bloom. This area was untouched by the timber companies because there is no profit in the cabbage tree or had they discovered the beauty of the red hearted wood of the cedar. The grasses growing along the river were now belly deep and the cows along with their calves were slick looking and healthy. Lize used his dogs to drive a small bunch of cows toward the others already gathered by Will and JT when an old steer with horns about six feet across turned and charged Lize. You need to understand, Lize was not a fast thinker and it took him some time to react to the rushing steer. Before he could turn and move out of the steer's way it caught Lize in the thigh. The horn ripped through his leg appearing he was speared to the horse. The horse first reaction was to free himself from the charging steer thus causing the gash to rip open striking a blood vein. Lize fell to the ground just as JT hit the steer the first time with his whip. In the confusion Lize's dogs caught the steer one by the nose and the other by the hind end. Lize lay still on the ground as Will pulled up sailing off his horse. The horse spooked to one side, quickly settling down and feeding on the tail grass. Lize fought against Will's assistance as he reached into his pocket. Pulling his pocket knife out and cutting away the slightly torn britches. Satisfied the steer would not charge again JT ran to his side and asked if he could help. Will spoke with a sense of firmness telling JT to calm Lize down, he was losing a lot of blood. JT began to speak to Lize in a tone trying to comfort a young child. Lize with glazed eyes focused on JT and began to ask if he was going to be ok. To which JT would assure him they were doing all they could but he needed to be calm as he rubbed his face. Lize relaxed clinching hard JT's hand. Tears rolled down the big man's face as he realized something was seriously wrong. Will whistled for his horse who quickly responded by coming to his side. He fumbled around in his wallet with blood soaked hands taking out a small bundle. Then moving toward the horse's tail and pulling a single strand of hair. Kneeling down Will removed the blood soaked bandana revealing a gabbing hole, clean through to the other side. By this time Lize had begun to slip in and out of consciousness due to the loss of blood. His breathing was becoming more labored as he began to lose hold of JT's hand. Will looked at JT desperate, shaking his head. Lize was fading fast and JT could not believe the speed a person could bleed out. Within seconds Lize was gone and a ton of logs hit JT in the chest. Years of time washed past him in only one second. Emotions he vowed he would never show again hit him. He stood quickly, taking several steps backward staring at the lifeless body of his brother in disbelief than looking at Will for some sort of explanation. Will stood and told JT he was sorry but the horn must have hit a vein ripping it open. It happened too fast and if they were able to get the bleeding to stop he probably would not have made the trip back to the hammock. JT asked, "What do we do now?" Will told him to stay put and he would go and get the others. He heard the sound of whips just north of where they were at and knew it to be Henry Lee and his crew. As Will rode off JT gathered Lize's stuff from the fallen horse and rolled Lize up in his slicker moving him from the stained ground. He sat down and began to cry. He did not cry this much when his mother whom he loved died. Every ounce of his strength was drained.

It seemed like hours before Will and the others returned. Henry Lee was the first to speak and complimented the memory of the young man lying dead before them. He told of his witness to his strength as they cut the hard heart of the tall lightered trees and assured JT the boy would be missed. Henry Lee and Elbert gently tied securing his body to the saddle for the two hour trip back to the creek. JT whistled for the dogs that sensed their beloved owner was dead and instinctively fell in behind JT's horse. They rode single file back through the cabbage trees that seemed to stand more erect as soldiers in honor of the dead that past, crossing Jim's Creek out into the scrub. Henry Lee and Elbert rode a head to pick up the cows near Settlement Slough and would meet the others back at Wills.

Finally the creek swamp came into view as JT rode up beside Will and said, "I don't know where I am going to bury him. We really don't have a home place anymore and I can't remember where ma and pa is buried." Will answers by giving permission for him to be buried at his place. To which JT mumbled a thankful reply.

He fell back in line behind Will as he watched his brother stretched across the saddle sway with each step the horse took. Henry Lee and Elbert were already back waiting for them to return. One of the Nettle's had started construction of a coffin out of some lumber he found in the barn.

Will and the others carried Lize to the back porch where JT undressed him and washed him. Taking the only other suit of clothes Lize owned from his wallet dressing him getting help from Henry Lee placed him in the coffin now sitting on the porch. Will insisted they take Lize into the kitchen area and lay him in wake in the kitchen and first thing in the morning they will bury him.

After sitting up with Lize all night JT walked out onto the front porch. The moon light bathed the clearing reflecting off the fog that had settled just above the ground and in the tops of the trees. Just outside of the touch of the light stood a figure, at first it startled JT thinking it was Lize but the figure was much smaller. It just stood there. JT's heart raced in his chest and his breath quickened. Then all of a sudden it just disappeared. Later that day he told Will about what he had seen who simply replied, "You seed a ghost".

CHAPTER 15

It took all of a week to gather all the Magrit cows and drove them to the newly fenced pastures. They had come across several men Will, Henry Lee or Elbert had never met. They were driving a small bunch of unmarked cows before them and told them they were from over close to the coast and it was getting harder to find wild cows these days. None of the three men spoke much and when they grew weary of listening to this stranger they simply dismissed themselves and rode off.

Henry Lee talked with JT this was the first time he could consider him human. He actually laughed and joked with JT. Then he walked over and spoke privately with Will. They said their final goodbyes and he loaded his horse into the back of his old pickup. He started to leave when he threw the truck into neutral got out of the truck and approached JT sitting next to Will on the front porch. He told him he was meeting his brother's Henry Lee and Will on the river marsh near Hat Bill to gather the rest of his cows. If he felt like it they would leave his place early Monday morning. If he wanted to come on Sunday he had a place for him to sleep. He could pay a lot but he would give him what he could. JT shook hands with Henry Lee and thanked him for the offer and promised if Mr. Magrit did not need him he would be there.

The following Sunday JT woke early. The sunrise was particularly bright that morning. Streaks of orange and red shot across the blue-gray sky. A slight fog hung just above the ground causing drops to fall like big rain drops. It was a morning which made you glad you were alive. He and Mr. Magrit spoke casually and shared a hot meal of fired fat back, hot biscuits and sweet potatoes. When the sun was above the horizon burning off the fog and had cleared the trees to the east JT walked halfhearted toward the small grave plot where he had buried the last of his kin. Standing there he heard the rustling of the bushes off to one side and saw one of Lize's dogs come into view. He noticed that the dog looked as if he himself was mourning the loss of his much-loved master much more the JT was. He hobbled over to the fresh turned dirt laying his head down ever so softly and simply quite breathing. He died right before JT's eyes. He knew he should bury him but he simply walked away leaving him where he lie. JT walked back to the front porch unsure of what he had just witnessed and to where he had earlier tied his horse. His heart hurt more than he ever thought it could. The emotions he had were overwhelming to him wishing he could understand them but life goes on. One of the saying Little John Nettle's always used now takes on new meaning, "Honey, you live till ya die". He said his goodbyes to Mr. Magrit and promised he would return as soon as he had fulfilled his obligation to Mr. Johnson.

Jibby Johnson was about six foot two inches tall and slender built with well defined muscles on his upper arms. He had dark sandy hair, a sort of pug nose and narrow eyes. He wore knee high boots that laced all the way up to his knees and always wore dark colored britches that flared out at the outer thighs. He is famous for wearing a small brim round dark hat. JT could count on his one hand the times he saw Jibby smile. He was a natural with horse. He was a man of uncommon strength, short temper and common since. He had little use for foolishness and could not tolerate stupidity.

JT was with him when a man named Bass tried to sell him a pretty good looking horse. The price was not equal to the horse and this caused Jibby to question what was wrong with the horse. He throws a saddle on the horse jumps on him and tears off. He runs the horse for about a quarter mile wheels him around causing the horse to lunge forward and opened him up. By the time he pulled up in front of Mr. Bass standing there with a sunned look on his face the horse was whistling so loud it echoed under the canopy of the large oak trees around the house. Jibby removed his saddle and handed the reins to old man Bass and walked away.

Henry Lee Johnson, Jibby's oldest brother was shorter more like their father. He owned his own place on the creek north of his father. He had an orange grove and a small dairy he and his wife milked ten cows twice a day. His wife, Aunt Billie would take several trips to Oviedo a week. Henry Lee was unable to see clear up close so he wears glasses. He sported a wide brim hat with a high top. Most of the time while working cows he wore leather chaps over light blue denim britches and denim long sleeve shirt. He would also spend weeks at a time on the St. John's River where the big creek dumped out just south of Lake Harney. All the boys were raised to love the outdoors but Henry Lee seemed to have a need to be outside.

Will, Jibby's second oldest brother looked a lot like Henry Lee in stature but his personality was lot easier going. Will was a people person and anyone who had ever met him for the first time instantaneously respected him for his honesty and candor. These are characteristic Henry Tanner their father instilled in each of his boys. He lived on the east side of the big creek half way between Henry Lee and their father. Will purchased a piece of property north of Horse Hammock later known as Wheeler Ranch.

JT straight away created a bond with the three Johnson brothers and learned to respect their skill on a horse and around cattle. He admires their proficiency in tracking and he was convinced that they almost knew what a hog, a deer or cow would do even before they did. Henry Lee and Will had several good dogs that were versatile used for both bear and hogs. They loved to hog hunt with a passion and enjoyed this pass time whenever they could break away from their daily chores.

Early Monday morning Jibby and JT waited for Henry Lee and Will at the goat house, the same place where Will Magrit grew up until he left at the age of fifteen on the St. Johns River. The reason why this particular place was called the goat house, the family that moved in after the Whaley's left tried to raise goats. After they realized they could not sell the stinking things they just abandoned them moving back up north. The goats just took over the house.

The Tanner's, along with the Simmons, Lee's, Kilby's, Osteen's and Tucker's ran their cows as far as Big Prairie. Big Prairie runs from just south of Cow Creek on the north east side of Lake Harney all the way to Titusville running south to Lake Washington, tree line to tree line.

The clanking and rattling of Henry Lee's wagon could be heard long before he actually entered the clearing in front of the barn. Jibby's horse turned his ears forward staring curiously in the direction of the noise. Clearing his throat Jibby stood from the bench in the shade of the front porch and walked to the edge leaning on one of the post. Bending slightly forward he looked out from beneath the eve of the house and commented about the weather making trying to casual conversation. A slight smile crossed his face as he caught the first glimpse of Henry Lee. In the back of his wagon he had his saddle straddling the supplies that would be needed for the next several days. "Hey, old brother" where the first words that shoot from Henry Lee's mouth as he climbed down from the wagon.

He continued by saying he was glad that JT was here because Will was not able to come this morning. He was called to Tanner Lake; which was later renamed Lake Nona. This was a camp Will would stay at and use as headquarters while working as Game Warden.

Will said, "He'll catch up with us at the next night's camp". Henry Lee looked irritated as he turned throwing his saddle up on the back of his horse that had calmed down after recognizing the noisy intruder as friendly. He jumped slightly being caught off guard but quickly calmed at the familiar touch of his master. Plans were to hunt to the west where Henry Lee had seen a few of their cows as he made his way here once gather then drive them back to the set of cow pens.

The three rode west through the thick switch-grass marsh spotted with small islands of towering cabbage trees. Every once in a while they would have to skirt around dense saw grass that even the heartiest and most rugged cowmen wants to avoid. The first bunch of cows ran and found refuge or what they thought was refuge in a deep willow pond about an acre in size. The dogs were given the signal to go and moved like torpedoes just under the surface of the tail switch-grass bursting free from their hiding catching the shifty cows off guard and by surprise. The chorus of dogs baying had always been music to JT. Every once in a while one would hear the bellow of an old cow being nipped by one of the many cure dogs commonly used as cow dogs, taking the refrain to an octave higher. Soon the annoyance would become too much the cow would then leave their hiding place seeking an open place to turn and fight. By this point the cowmen would move in with their long whips undone, reaching out and harshly touching the cow sending patches of hair and hide. By this time the sound of working cows had reached its zenith. To the unskilled this would seem like a time of confusion but to the trained cowman it was the beginning of a good day. The barking of dogs, the lowing of cattle and the echo of the cracking of the long whips bouncing off the towering cabbages trees may seem as just noise of some but to the cowmen is the ballet of their existence, a source of pleasure and affirmation even though it is hard work. Along with gratification in a way of life that is quickly fading for so many.

Henry Lee rode on the south side of the small bunch of cows keeping them as bunched as possible while Jibby rode on the north side and JT trailed behind. JT watched with amazement how the Johnson brother controlled their dogs. The dogs trotted at the feet of their horse's one eye on the cows and the other on the man in the saddle. Each had an understanding of the consequences for any infraction no matter how small. JT quickly learned the punishment for breaking the rules. With a quick and lighten fast response Jibby sent the sixteen foot cow whip popping it hitting the dog on its hind end. It took only once for the dogs to realize their place and with tails tucked they resumed their place at the horse's feet.

JT thought he was the first to notice the tail figure of a man atop a horse in front of the gate at the cow pens but Jibby saw him ride from the south out of a break in the cabbage hammock bordering the big creek. He recognized him as being Will Magrit and welcomed his help in this endeavor of gathering the cows and moving them to their home pasture. The men even though they were good friends only tipped their hat at each other understanding the need to finish this push before any pleasantries could be spoken.

The gate swung open as Will Magrit rode off to one side giving the still wild and unruly cows plenty of room. The wild look in their eyes was sign their work was not finished until they had every one of them securely in the pan and the big gate closed. The lead cows was a crazy banana horned brindle red cow. She offered to catch Henry Lee but was persuaded different when the whip reached out and touched her on the end of the nose. She stops shakes her head in disbelief her bluff was not taken serious. Just as the last of the cows were making their way into the pen a yearling bull wheeled to run. His intent was to break free but there stood one obstacle in his way and that was Jibby. Immediately the dogs were in hot pursuit nipping and biting at his heels. Finally one managed to get in front, leaping it latched onto the nose of the bull. Twisting his body in mid air the bull flipped landing on his side, without any effort the bull was back on his feet heading back in the direction he had just come and without any more persuading he found the gate and hide among the others. The cow pens were filled with head high dog fennels and thick stands of myrtles which had grown since the last time they worked cows here. The cows promptly calmed as they ate the grasses covering the ground.

Will Magrit told the men he had sighted a bunch of cows with a "T" on their right shoulder as he passed through Horse Hammock close to the Nettles hog pen. He mentioned several looked really poor for this time of year. They followed him as he led them back toward Orange Mound. Finding fresh *sign* (a cracker word meaning the tracks of the animal) as far as Near Slough where they found seven very thin cows wondering aimlessly, almost blind. The sight troubled the men. JT could see it on their faces than without another word Jibby pulls his rifle without looking at the others who were doing the same. The silence of the hammock exploded with the bang, bang, bang, of rifle shot halting as quickly as it started as the last of the cows stumbled and fell. The sight sickened the men who busied themselves with the task of piling and burning the dead cows.

Without another word they turned and headed toward Blues Head so they could cross the river with ease. They rode without a word knowing this was going to be the norm until the dreaded fever was brought under control. Stopping at Paw-Paw Mound for the noon meal they were joined by some of the Platt and Cox riders. They reported the same news as Will shared. Recognizing Henry Lee they told him they too had kill six of his cows close to Possum Bluff. Henry Lee looked at Jibby and spoke with a sense of urgency in the necessity of getting this chore done as quickly as possible or they would have no cows left. One of the Platt hunters told of the plans for building a vat for dipping their cattle but they are trying to put it off as long as possible.

JT had heard talk of dipping vats but was unsure how they actually worked so he sat in the shadows listening as the men talked. He noticed an anger rise in some as they spoke of having to dip their cattle. The schedule for dipping was once every fourteen days. This would first put a hardship on all cowmen especially the ones who had smaller herds. They fear they would have to get rid of their cows or they will all die. Some depended upon their cows as the only source of income while others had different means of income which meant they could not take away from one of their ventures without the other being hindered. The next difficulty they spoke of was who will police the dipping. To which one of the Cox riders spoke telling of how there are men from the capital looking for local riders to hire as "*Range Riders*" (these were local men hire to by the State to enforce the mandatory dipping). Their duties would include riding the woods killing deer and any other fur bearing animals and watch out for sick cows. Their main responsibility is to be present for the dipping. Henry Lee stood abruptly his demeanor completely changed as he said, "Ani't no one telling me what I can do with my cows". He walked toward his horse placing his hand on the back of the saddle then turning back again he continued. "You mean they's wants us to make sure each other is doen' what they tell us to do. A man can get shot sticken' his nose in another man's business. That's a damn sight, ani't it?" No one said a word in answer because they felt the same as Henry Lee. Finally Jibby spoke and said he was thinking about doing it because times are hard and he and his family could use the extra money. Henry Lee along with the others were surprised by his declaration and he was about to chastise him when Jibby finished his statement. "But, it wouldn't be round here I'll do it. I have too many friends around here to force another to kill or sell his cows, if he don't want to". A chorus of resolved voice joined in agreement with him.

I feel I must interject here letting the reader know at this point in history the progression of the cattle industry in Florida will forever change. Up to this point in time whether a man owned one head or one thousand head of cattle he was called a 'Cowman". Families did not see their neighbor as owning or having more then another. All men were equal in the pre-dipping era. Families would help families with no questions asked. But after this era men who were once friends are now leery of each other. Deep grooves were edged as deep as fire lines that scare the landscape lasting for generations. Their effects still hurt today.

Chapter 16

December 1920

By this time most of the cowmen had seen the affects of this small invader and began trying to abate this present difficulty. Like always they faced this danger head on never backing down from any challenge. There was not one family untouched by what was happening. Many had lost a third of their herds. Some were forced to sell out to those willing to take the gamble. Many of the new owners allowed those who could to continue to work the cows trying to help those who had felt the pain of this time. Some out of necessity became "Ranger Riders".

Not only the wild cattle population suffered but where you could once see massive herds of wild horses and deer you will be lucky to see only a handful. The depletion of the deer population due to the pestilent caused many families to go hungry because they depended upon the deer and cattle. Children who would have survived now fill the family plots. Bitterness settled across the state and many looked for someone to blame.

Wild hogs were not affected by the tick and ignored. Many of the onetime cowmen began herding hogs driving them to the nearest market trying to continue to exist. A cracker never killed for the pleasure but out of necessity to feed his family or to make a little extra money. Now he could not or dare not pass one deer up for fear that particular one carries the tick that could infect him, his family or his stock.

January 1921

The cold wind blew early in the morning causing the branches of the oaks to move in time with its whistling. The constant scraping of a lower limb against the tin roof started to irritate Will Magrit as he waits patiently for the sun to rise beyond the horizon. Streaks of light drove their way through the thick growth of trees. He steadily paces back and forth from the stove as he keeps a vigil over the coffee pot and the front door as he waits for the arrival of the day. He had been awake for several hours, putting on the second pot of coffee. The fire in the stove chased the cool of the night away as he contemplated the day's chores. The dogs barked franticly bring him to the front porch. He gazed out into the darkness when he heard the harsh stern voice of the riders quieting the dogs. To his surprise Jibby, Elbert and Emmett rode into the clearing. The moon was waning yet it cast enough light for the men to ride along the scrub unhindered. The news the men were to deliver could not wait any longer. The commotion outside awakened JT with a start causing him to sit right up in bed grabbing franticly for his pistol, Will laughed telling him to get up. The front room now filled with casual conversation. It was not until JT came shuffling from his room he realized what was going on.

For the past several weeks JT had been riding the new fence at night due to it being cut by someone. Will is not sure of whom it is that keeps cutting his fence but he is determined to win this battle without having to go back to the old way hunting the violator down and deal with them once and for all. Evil men are like mad dogs there is only one cure if you know what he means.

JT hopes to find them committing the act of vandalism or happen upon their came because he was getting tired of repairing what they destroy. He had not slept an entire night since starting this nightly routine. This is the reason why he came dragging his feet and was not already awake when the others arrived.

Elbert told of what he learned while visiting his family in Crab Grass. The state had determined the Texas Tick Fever so bad that every cow in Florida whether it is wild or domestic will have to be dipped every fourteen days. The news did not surprise Will because he felt this was coming, his only concern was what would the first step to compliance be? Jibby told of the plans to build four vats in the area. The first will be built on the big creek near Cow Pen Branch. The next will be built on the big creek further north on Big Prairie. Another will be located at Pee Tree Branch (*on the old*

Stone Ranch). And the last will be built on the south east corner of Lake Hart atop the sand ridge near Bear Island (*present day Moss Park*). These locations are believed to be convenient and will not place a hardship on the cowmen of the area. They set a date for two weeks to meet at Cow Pen Branch and build the first of the four vats.

February 1921

Will and JT decided to head toward Big Prairie the day before the set day. There was no telephone or daily contact between the cowmen so they would set dates almost a year ahead and if they give their word they counted on each other to show up. The reason for their decision was so they could get a good night's rest. The first item of business was to dig a trench three and a half feet wide, six foot deep and eighteen feet long so they could frame to pour concrete. Even though it was cool the men sweated as they pushed the dull shovels and spades into the hard soil and thick roots of the small oak hammock chosen to build the vat. It took all of the first day and most of the next for the last shovel of dirt was thrown from ditch. Immediately the carpenters stepped in and framed the four inch walls. It rain the night before they were able to hand mix the concrete. By the sixth day the concrete had hardened the holding pens were built out cypress post freshly cut from the cypress head to the west. Langdon Hatch delivered rough cut boards from Sanford on his launch, a welcomed sight because it meant fresh meat. They were loaded on a wagon at the mouth of Puzzle Lake and hauled it back to the spot of the vat. When it was finished the men knew they needed to move to the next location but needed to gather supplies so they would have no delay in the next project.

It took a month to complete the four dipping vats, each got easier because they learned from their past mistakes. While finishing the last on Pee Tree Branch news arrived that a vat was dynamited south of Kissimmee and four men were killed in a fierce gun battle protecting the work and their livelihood. With this news, not one man was too far from his rifle. While Will Tanner visited their camp near Pee Tree Branch he told the story of Nehemiah in the Bible. Because of their enemy some worked while others stood by with spears and swords. Most looked strangely at him but understood what he meant by the comparison.

As soon as the last nail was driven, the last bucket of water scooped from the nearby source, hauled by ox wagon and poured into the vat and a strong solution of arsenic was just right the task of gathering the cattle started. Will Magrit made arrangements with other cowmen in the area to drive his cows to Cow Pen Branch. They paid close attention to keep the cows bunched as close as possible to avoid coming in contact with any cow in the open range.

The gate swung open as the riders slipped into and around the cows nervously moving in the pen holding the last bunch of Magrit cows started moving. Will Magrit examines each cow as it passes noticing a few were sickly looking but he believed it to be caused by the lack of good grass rather than the fever. After the last cow finally left the pen JT saw a small calf huddled next to the fence too weak to lift its head. Reaching down he lifted the small calf in front of him and rode out into the palmettos. He set the calf under the shade of a myrtle, pulled his pistol, aimed and pulled the trigger. His horse threw its head up and down in objection to the surprise blast. It sickened JT to have to kill the calf but knew sacrificing a few was better than losing the entire herd.

The echo of the cracking and popping of whips bounced off the scrub oaks and towering pines along the trail and the lowing of nerves cows could be heard a mile away. It had not rained in several days and the pounding of hundreds of hooves caused a hovering cloud of dust, slowly in moved across the yellow green palmetto fans disappearing into nothingness. There seemed to be a since of urgency in the days task. Absent was the teasing and relaxed attitude of past hunts even thought JT and the others knew this was unlike any of the drives they had been on before. The last of the cows reluctantly entered the newly constructed pen.

The first rider to meet them was a stranger. He was about six feet three inch tall and Jibby said he looked like a pine sapping. The only thing holding his britches up was a shoddy pair of suspenders. His hat was small brimmed and high atop. The reason for his presence was to verify that each cow will be dipped. His name is Tom Small from over around Bartow. JT really like the old man learning his family had been in Florida for over a hundred years. He spoke with a long draw and so slow, never getting excited about anything. His easiness and speed annoyed the Tanner brothers. It aggravated Henry Lee so bad he finally had to leave before he did something he ought not to do.

Will Magrit stands at the end of the vat where the cows exited and dabbed paint on the shoulder of the cows. The reason for this was the Ranger Riders could ride through cows in the scrub and see they had been dipped. It did not take long for this routine to get old and the men grew weary.

Chapter 17

March 1922

For one year, every fourteen days, rain or shine they had gathered the cows. JT was now riding his third horse. His first horse had several ticks and died within a week. JT agrees the horse was not in the best of shape because having to be in the saddle everyday of the week. The next horse was a young filly that died as the result of arsenic burn and her belly splitting open, let me explain. Every piece of livestock had to be dipped. After the last cows were run through then the cowmen would remove their saddles and run the horses, mules and oxen through. JT allowed his horse to drip dry on the small pad of concrete used to keep the runoff from contaminating the ground. Thunderclouds darkened the sky and the thunder rolled in the southwest. Just as JT cinched his saddle and swung atop her it started to rain. This down pour drenching him and the horse in just seconds. The problem was the rain stopped and disappeared as sudden as it appeared causing the arsenic to wash to the horse's belly and when the sun came out it got hot. The result was the belly of the horse split open. JT did not notice the split until he rode up next to Henry Lee and he noticed all the blood. Immediately he climbed down and carefully removed the saddle dropping it down by his side. The small filly turns trying to avoid the pain it had been in for hours. She would turn her head biting at the largest open sore when JT withdrew his pistol and at point blank range pulled the trigger. Instantly the small horse fell to its side, kicking just once before it lay still. JT walked about one hundred yards and set camp up under a small stand of oaks. Henry Lee rode away heading for the Magrit place to get a replacement. They were about two days ride from there so JT killed a small doe cutting the back strap out and placing it in the bottom of a dutch-oven. While he explored his surroundings he discovered wild onions and adding the last of the potatoes he had in his wallet he placed the pot on the fire. He had gathered several small pieces of lightered and figured he could place the pot on the fire and explore around the scrub but he was wrong because it took all of his time watching the pot. He created a greater respect for the women who were camp cooks. He thought it difficult riding and punching wild cows out of the lower swamps and thick scrubs but learned fixing meals and doing camp chores were harder.

Just before dark he heard the lone cry of a wolf deep in the creek swamp. It continued until late in the night. He had never heard such a mournful cry but the fear it caused quickly replaced any sympathy he may have felt as it got closer and closer. The moon was hidden by the fast moving clouds that threatened rain. The flash of lightening followed by the rumble of thunder sent a shiver up his spine as he drew closer to the fire. He never feared the darkness nor did he mind being alone without a horse.

One thing JT enjoyed was the stories he would tell. Looking out into the dark scrub; the only light is the lightening that streaks across the sky from east to west illuminating the towering pines. One particular story was about a Seminole Indian he often saw gliding upon the dark waters of the creek. JT recalls his father telling him he was awestruck by his size and wardrobe. A shudder courses through his body caused by the possibility of one day seeing such a sight and wondering if he would be friend or enemy. The wolf howls again and this time he was a lot closer than last time. Tossing another piece of lightered that quickly brought the small fire to its fullness.

He had fond memories of his mother. He remembers her occasional acts of love but never remembers her telling him that she loved him. He vowed if he was ever blessed with a family he would tell his children often of his love for them. He rolls out his bed checking it for spiders. Then he sits and pulls his boots off folding them over and placing the next to the head of his bed for fast access just in case he needed them. There still was a slight chill in the air and with the moisture from the passing rain it seemed colder than what it actually was. Just as he started to lie down the wolf howled again and this time he was in the shadows just beyond the reach of the fire. This really bothered JT because this means he slipped by him without him hearing and the thought was eerie to him. All of a sudden the call of nature came he tried to ignore it as long as he could. He stands walks to the edge of camp and begins his business when he looked across a small switch grass pond and saw the glow of another camp fire. He drops to his knees and crawls back to his fire tossing handfuls of sand trying hard to extinguish the flame and hide the light when out of the darkness he heard the voice of a stranger speak from behind him. With the small amount of light cast by the remaining fire he could only see the figure of a man standing next to a tall pine tree. His first response to this intruder was to take his eyes off of him and look directly at his rifle he had foolishly left next to his bed, a mistake he will never make again. Finally the man moves from the shadows picks up a piece of lightered gently placed it on the fire and squats next to it. His gestures were friendly and there seemed to be something familiar about this stranger. He could tell by his clothes and his dark skin and sharp features that he was an Indian. Immediately JT relaxed and this bothered him. Another thing bothering him was the old Indian sat next to his rifle placing himself between himself and his rifle. JT knew this was not a mistake but assured the visit was friendly because if he meant him harm he could have already done it.

They sat in silence as they watched the flames casting its light creating figures and shapes that danced in the trees surrounding the camp. JT offered him foot but was rejected. The first words came from the old Indians mouth as he pointed up into the trees and said, "There is the wolf". His words caused JT to spring to a standing position because he feared the wolf he had heard earlier and without fear now enters the camp. The old Indian smiles shaking his head and says "No, look there in the trees. The fire has cast the shape of a wolf running. He is the last of the wolves." His voice faded as he continued, "Just as I am the last of my people". With piercing eyes he stared at JT and said, "You too are the last of your kind."

Author's notes- (For years there has been a struggle between the native Indians of Florida and the strangers who happened to be interested in the land at any particular time. The Spaniards, the French and the British Dragoons had all tried unsuccessfully to force their will upon the Indian. The great conflicts between the newly formed United States of America and the natives was about to erupt. The end result will be as the last. More promises are made then broken without a blink of an eye. The Indian became more distrustful, cautious and watchful. Their clans are forced to retreat even further into the dense swamp south of the big lake. The great tribes had to disband into family clans of twenty to thirty-five members in order to survive the harsh and unforgiving area. They learned to survive by eating morsels grubbed from the earth, eating the turtle and gar fish and using the cattail as flour. Salt was gathered from burning palmetto roots, scrapping the white crystals which form from the dew and boiling to separate the life preserving mineral. Once they owned large herds of cattle, hogs and horses now forced to depend on others for the daily rations of life.)

A prophesy, born out of necessity. If there is nothing to hope in then their people will perish. Tuc-ma of the Otter clan carved a spear with special markings clearly definable. He started with his own clan and told of how the Great Spirit appeared to him. Telling him there was coming One who will lead their people, while holding this spear. It will be lost for a while but he will come. The news spread like a wild fire and hope began to spring from the ashes of despair. No one ever saw Tuc-ma again but the prophecy still lives until today.

Chapter 18

JT sat across from the old Indian the only light was the flicker of the
light from the fire. He could see in his eyes a tiredness he saw once in his
father's eyes and that was the night he passed away. The anxiety of their
first meeting subsided the longer they sat together when finally the old man
spoke. "Is that your horse in the woods that is dead?" JT shock his head
affirming his question explaining what happened. They spoke of what he
had seen while traveling from south Florida. He spoke of his concerns and
how the once vast herds of cattle had disappeared. He told of watching
sick cows south of Kissimmee. He spoke of a place his people once called
Sick Cow Island. JT shook his head because he had once heard of the
place south of Fort Drum. To him it was all too strange because he could
not understand their actions. JT shrugs his shoulders because he too was
still trying to understand what his part will be with the cattle after all of
this comes to an end. JT reaches for the steaming pot of coffee offering
the old man a cup of which was accepted they sipped on the black liquid
satisfyingly. The clouds broke a quarter moon sent what light it could into
the darkness of the night. The old man stood struggling to maintain his
balance he leaned on the staff he carries. As he turned JT saw the long
knife hanging at his side. He commented as the old man smiled touching
it with reverence saying we will speak in the morning then disappears into
the darkness.

Sleep came slow for JT as he thought of his encounter with a real
Seminole Indian. There was something familiar about the large knife. It
resembled the one he was given by his father just before he died. Just before
he fell asleep he heard for the last time the fading call of the lone wolf as

he seemed to be searching for another of his kind but to no avail. JT felt sorry for the once declared enemy of the cowman wishing him well. His night was filled with dreams of what it must have been like when his father and the old Indian were boys.

The sun rises in the east. It projected its beams of orange-red tint upon the clouds. The morning was a welcomed sight for two reasons. First, Henry Lee should return today and he could get back to doing what he loved more than his time alone in the woods, then for the opportunity to see the old Indian and hear his story.

Just as the sun cleared the horizon the old man come shuffling into camp without make any noise. JT was amazed the old man at his age was able to bear the burden of his pack. They sat together sharing the remaining stew from the night before when the old man began to share his story.

"I believe the year was 1834 deep in the woods of south Florida I was born". No mid-wife, no doctor, no fanfare, just the birth of a baby boy. My mother, a member of the Otter Clan of the Seminole Indians slips from her Chickee at the first pains of birth. The birth of a child in her world was celebrated but secret, considered just another chore of everyday life for Seminole women. Determined she steadies herself as she heads toward the gently flowing creek not far from her camp. Days before she found a tree she would use in aiding with the birth. She approached the chosen spot uncovers the bundle of deer hide she placed there in preparation for this moment. She stops leans hard against the small cedar, using it for stabilizing her as she squats. The pain now is so strong it almost takes her breath. She tries to relax but the pain strikes hard as she loses her balance and rolls to her side. Tradition has taught her baby will die if she lies at this time so she summons all her strength rights herself by taking hold of the sapling pulling herself back to a squatting position.

This practice helps her to assist nature when the actual time of birth came. Seminole Indian women never cried out in child birth and very few ever needed help at this time. She now notices her feet wet. As the pain intensifies, it now is so great she shakes the young tree letting escape from her lips an agonizing but muffled moan. Then it happened in just a single moment. The baby drops to the soft deer moss covered by the hair side of a deer skin. Quickly the baby is scooped into his mother's arms sucking at her breast.

She spends the next few hours holding her baby, counting and recounting his perfect fingers and toes. He eats several times while she rests allowing her body to adjust to this new role as mother. Finally, she stands, wraps her joy in the soft deer skin, and walks back toward her camp. She looks into the sky noticing the dark rolling clouds and feels the brisk cold wind. She chants words to the Great Spirit, thanking Him and asking His care for her son. She and her husband name the boy James.

"Before I was born my parents had befriended a Baptist Missionaries who came to the wilderness to minister to the Seminole Indians." They were from a small settlement named Cortz in Hillsborough County. His name was Simmons. The missionary was a kindly man standing about six foot three inches tall, slender, with white hair. His mustache covered his upper lip hanging down to his chin. He was a gentle man and kindly. His manner was what gave his message life. His wife only stood five foot three inches tall and wore her hair in a bun on top of her head. She fancied the brightly colored dresses the Seminole Indian women wore and proudly wore their native dress as a way to prove her sincerity. She had lost her leg while saving her youngest child from a rattlesnake and that is why she walks with a limp. Their purpose for coming was to see if they could deliver the heathen from their sin.

James' father and mother were gentle people as well. They were intrigued by the words spoken by this gentle man. They watched his words translate into actions. James' parents wanting to hold to the traditions of their people but knew there was more to life and found it in the words these strange people spoke. He spoke of a man named Jesus, the Son of God who died because we do wrong and he loved us. Everything their people did to provoke them they faced with a strength they had never known. Even at the loss of a child was faced with a greater power than that of the Medicine Man. If this God who had acted so strangely could do this He must be real so they embraced Him. In doing so they became out cast.

"In the village where I was raised lived an old medicine man who labored hard to convince everyone the white man could not be trusted. Nightly he would tell stories of the three wars. How his people were hunted like animals. How many were sent away to die on the barren lands to the west.

He related stories of how poor the land was the weeds could not even live most of the year. As in Florida they could not own cattle or hunt the deer without being seen as thieves. A man was reduced to nothing more than a dog. How the white man would kill anything that was alive without regard for anything.

Some listened and believed and many learned to hate and distrust anyone born white.

"My father believed he could find good, in all men whether they be red or white and he taught me the same. He stood against the medicine man, careful not to be seen standing against the traditions the medicine man taught. The result was my family being driven from the camp."

The sun rose the first morning after they had to leave their camp. James had never seen such a brilliant sight in his entire life. The bright amber glow fading into a deep blue helped to relieve the sting they felt by the rejection. They traveled for hours without a word arriving in the small cabbage hammock after dark. A hammock his father had visited many times as a child. The old chickee's sagged because it had been abandoned many years before. Later he would learn this was the sight of one of the most brutish massacres in Seminole War history. James's father feared telling his mother because of her superstition. James could hear his parents arguing in their native language as his mother for the first time in James' young life openly disagreed with his father. He could only make out small bits of their conversation but one thing he was sure of his mother wanted to return and allow her son to be raised as she was. Deep inside James' heart he wishes the same thing. He felt his father was denying him his birth right and wanted to tell him so, but feared his father too much. He had experienced his wrath and bore the scares to prove just how cruel he could be. James slips from his bed and steps out into the cool breeze that must have started during the night. He shivers, returns to his bed and retrieves a deer skin jacket his mother had made him from the skin of his first deer. He is overwhelmed by pride as he finally experiences its warmth and can wear it comfortably. He turns in the dim light of the morning admiring the bright colors, wishing his friends could see this prize. Again he steps into the clearing and is in awe of what he sees. There must be at least ten chickee's off to one side of the clearing. He noticed pumpkins lying among large brown leaves. Wanting to distance himself from the conflict in his parent's chickee he takes a trail behind one of the larger structures. In and through the grape vines blanketing the trail he struggles to climb atop the vines. Able only to crawl across them when he finally was finally on the other side he again was overwhelmed by what he saw. There before him was an actual burial mound. He circled the mound awestruck at its massive size then approaches with reverence. He places his hands upon a sandy spot laying his head down trying hard to hear the story of those resting there. His mind imagined many things. The battles he fought in his thoughts seemed so real to the boy his breath increased and the pounding of his heart filled his ears. So lost in the moment he was unaware his father had followed him to this spot and stood watching trying hard to understand the actions of his son. At last he steps forward startling James when he abruptly rolls to a sitting position and stares fearfully at his father. He sits down on a log near him and calls for his son to come and sit next to him. James looks at his father confused and asked what this all meant. Lost in the moment he began to tell of the time when their family lived in this hammock and life was good. This is the place where he and his mother were born and grew up until the cruel white man came and killed one hundred of his family.

"My father's grandfather went out hunting. By going he escaped the initial attack and when they returned they found men, women and children slaughtered. The small herd of cattle we used to supplement the deer and hogs they could gather from the surrounding scrub and lower swamps were gone. He told me of how they worked for days preparing the dead for burial. The only way this could be done before the buzzards found them was to pile and place the earth over them. On the third day while filling the many baskets with dirt great-grandfather touched his shoulder then placed his finger to his mouth and motioned for me to follow. They then hide and watched as a handful of women and small children emerged from the thick palmettos into the clearing. They recognized those who escaped as they returned from their hiding place. They again wept for those who had died and worked together to complete the burial".

The old man looked into JT eyes telling him the place he speaks of is not far from where they sit and holds good memories and bad.

"I remember looking to my father mystified and asked why would men do this kind of thing to other men? He looked off into the distance and spoke the word greed".

In their native tongue they had no word for their meanness. Then they sat in deafening silence. His last words as they left the mound was out of respect for their ancestors they touched nothing and left everything as it was before the attack.

Together they returned to the camp. James' mother had prepared one of the pumpkins and fried some of the hog his father had killed the day before. They sat silently and enjoyed her labor of love. There was plenty of game here and his father saw no reason to continue on their journey for a few days. James explored the camp and found a knife buried under the ashes of one of the ckeckee's and asked his father if he could have it. His father spoke harshly to him about disturbing the dead as he stuck out his hand taking the knife. The moment it touched his hand he recognized the knife as belonging to his father and said so, dropping it in the dirt. "This is the knife I still carry".

He bends so he can take hold of the handle of the knife slipping the huge knife from its deer skin sheath handing it to JT. As fast as he pulled his JT had his out catching the glare of the sun as it breaks through the shade of the trees. His swiftness startled the old man and when JT realized his action could be taken threatening he apologized as he recoiled dropping the knife at the old man's feet. With a steady hand the old man reached down scoops up the knife admiring it looking back in the past when he said. "I have seen this knife before." He pauses gazing off as if he was drawing from some deep reserve. His eyes brighten as he turns to JT and says. "It was on the big creek not far from here. I was moving north on the creek when I heard a man cough. He was bad sick, coughing up blood. I stopped and help the man. I stayed with him for three days until he regained his strength. He thanked me and I acted as if I could not understand him. I believe his name was like one of the men in the words the preacher spoke. With a uncertain look on his face he spoke as almost asking. "Malachi?" I would know this even if my mind had not faded so much. JT dropped to his knees before the old man. He was shocked his expression and action concerned the old man until JT told him that he was talking about his father. From that moment on there seemed to be a bond that transcends both age and heritage.

The old man began again telling his story. "I bent over picking up the knife turning it over and over finding a new meaning and pride to the old sooty knife". The sunlight glistened in the tear as it rolls down his father's cheek. He turns disappearing into the woods. James carries the knife to the small spring using the coarse white sand begins to rub away the rust and smut revealing a shiny gray blue steal. James cherished the knife and spoke to his mother about his longing to have something so grand especially because it once belonged to his grandfather he had never meant. His mother told him to give his father time and he will probably change his mind.

That afternoon his father called for James to follow him. They went into the woods. Curiously he watched as his father searched for the right small cedar sapling he could used to replace the handle of the knife burnt in the fire. His father took this time to teach James how their people would carve out the wooden grips. Making them to fit their hand, then he showed to him how they would wrap the handle with deer skin strips. How they use to sharpen the knives. How to use the well balanced knife once it was restored. That night James' dreams were filled with adventure lying for hours waiting impatiently for the first sign of day light so he could practice again.

The next morning he was awakened by the noise of rustling next to the sleeping chickee startling him. This caused him to sit straight up in bed. His first reaction was to grab for his knife. Still half asleep he managed to ease to the edge allowing him to peer out. Not knowing if the nefarious white men had returned to finish the job they had started so many years before. He relaxed relieved when he saw next to the chickee a wren scratching, darting and making all sort of noise as she went. Amused, James watched as it raced from one bug to the next as it fought with the obstruction. He watched as she moved slowly without being harassed by anything, unaware any stranger had invaded their world. He watched until she disappeared into the thick undergrowth of young cabbage trees, cedars and wild oranges trees surrounding the clearing. In the distance he heard the call of the whooping crane. While on their way here they spent one entire afternoon watching the Malachiing ritual of the whooping crane as the males competed for the favor of their Malachie. With little effort their wings extended out as they would leap three to four feet into the air all the while bobbing their head this was a majestic sight. as they leaped and bobbed their long heads tying hard to win the slightest glance from the female that did not seem interested. James determined the call of the crane was forlorn, one he could not compare with any other. Also he was amazed that such a relatively small bodied bird could be heard from such a long distance away.

Setting his knife down within arms distance he vigilantly started dressing. Deep inside, he senses something out of the ordinary. A feeling he had before but cannot understand. Taking a long cedar stick he steps from the shelter hoping not to encounter the pigmy rattlesnakes his father warned him about. Needing to relieve his self forgetting about the wren shuffling his feet in the dim light he flushed her from her hiding place startled by the flurry of wings and the cracking of cabbage fans. When you are not prepared, a sound like that catches you off guard as it did James. He wildly swings the stick. Realizing what happened he was embarrassed and chuckled at himself glad no one was around to see his reaction. Thinking to his self how stupidly he was as he caught sight of the last of the little wrens scurry for cover. His heart beats hard in his chest as he takes a deep breath to clear his mind.

After they had eaten together James and his father walked to the open spans of water bordered by the willow tree. One corner of the pond was covered with bonnets covered with white blooms. Using a long spear his father began teaching him the art of fishing Seminole style. James strains to see the large bass as it swims just below the surface of the water. With lightening speed the spear plunges into the water then lifting it just above the surface revealing the bass. James finally understood what his father was trying to teach him and what he was to look for. From that time forward James would see the fish before his father. James gladly took the responsibility of providing fresh fish when he was asked. Before his father left standing in knee deep water his father warned him about the keeping his eyes open for the sneaky alligator.

"My father began to drills me in the use of the knife, demonstrating how to hold it in combat and how to throw it. After killing a fat maiden doe he instructed me as to how to skin the deer. I loved the old knife as much as anyone could love just a thing. My mother used the skin of the first deer he dressed to make this sheath. It is decorated with bright beads and shells. The die is faded now because it was many years ago. I proudly wore the knife only removing it when I slept or swam".

CHAPTER 19

With each passing summer James grows taller and stronger. His skin tanned brown. His high cheek bones made him a striking picture of pure Seminole Indian. His father beams with pride as James becomes proficient with the bow and arrow. He only had to be shown once on how to assembly the arrows. He is fierce with the old knife. Whatever stood still long enough within twenty feet was dead! "Once I proudly walked into the camp holding a rabbit I had killed while on the run. I was so excited and I told my father the entire hunt. I shared every detail of how I slipped through the tail grass without being detected". His father surprised him when he did not share in his enthusiasm.

I was confused and asked father if I had done wrong. I could not understand why he did not compliment me for my skill. When father set me down and explained to me I should not kill anything unless I can use it. He went on by telling me that we have plenty and this rabbit will go to waste if we do not eat it. My father told me to clean it and give it to mother. She would fix it for my supper. I learned a lesson and from that day forward I never killed without a purpose".

James' ability to track and kill the buck far surpassed his father's. As his father and mother grew older he will be able to provide for them. "We grew comfortable in the hammock of our ancestors".

After gaining permission James was allowed to explore to the outer boundaries of the large hammock. He found a grove of thirty dwarf cypress trees. Even though they were only about twenty feet high they were about twenty feet around. While on one of his trips James saw some cow hunter. These were the first white men he had ever seen. One night

James stayed longer than usual at his favorite fishing hole when he spotted the glare of a campfire as its light danced on the a pine island east of the hammock. Inquisitive he quietly slipped through knee deep water and positioned himself in a spot so he could watch the men sitting at the fire. He could not fully understand their conversation but was confused these men who were so cruel could laugh as much as they do. After returning to camp he told his father about what he had seen. His father told him not all white men were as callous as some but he needed to be careful trying to get close to them. During certain times of the year the cow hunters ventured closer and closer to their camp and by all the stories his father have told him he feared them.

Summer pasted and fall begins to show its self when James's father entered the camp telling his mother they will be leaving soon. He is growing weary of having to drive the cows away from their hammock fearing becoming discovered. James asked why it is so important to not have the cows near their hammock when his father told him where there are cows there will be cow hunters. They could not afford to have their camp discovered.

While James was exploring the neighboring hammock he discovered two dug-outs. He and his father worked together fixing a crack in one. These will be used to escape if the hunters happened to find them.

Early one morning they placed all they possessed in the canoes and began to make their way through the saw grass marsh situated between Cox Creek and Lake Toho near Kissimmee. This open marsh ran for miles to the northwest ending near a small settlement called Narcoossee. The marsh merged into several small lakes to which they would stick close to the shore as they made their way further north. James watched closely taking into account the many details just in case he would have to one day return this way by himself. The small open water trail snaked through large open spans of water cover with the lily pads. When his mother would tire he would stand awkwardly at first poling the dug out with great effort. His arms oozed blood caused by scrapping across the saw-grass. His sweat washed over the cuts causing them to burn along with the aching in his arms and legs tortured him. His father watched as James would begin to lag behind so he would stop pointing out things allowing him to rest without harming his pride.

Their destination is a small grove of dwarf cypresses on the northeast shore of a large clear lake. Even though it is located between two growing settlements very few people knew this place existed. To James it was if they had passed into another world. Even fewer would dare to cross the deep marsh surrounding the lake. There were several natural savannahs running through the marsh but if you were not careful you would make a wrong turn and end up at a dead end. James' father had told him when their people first come here long ago many of them died while learning this particular marsh. He warmed him to be careful making note of every tree and bush so he would not make a mistake. If you did not know what you were doing you would think you were walking on grass when in truth it was large floating islands. His father learned this as a small child when he watched a large bull carelessly venture too far, falling through and quickly drowning.

This place was once a camp for his family and he knew there would be plenty of game for them to survive. Here James' father can help to sharpen his son's skills. Helping to make him a man for this new world he knew was coming. They will have to adapt or fade away. His father is determined that his son will live to tell the tale of his people.

James did not like this reclusive lifestyle. His days were consumed with thoughts of returning to the camp of his birth. His nights were filled with dreams of running and fishing with boys his age. He tried to imagine what the other boys now looked like and if they would remember him. He wondered if they were learning from their fathers as he. He would take long trips into the scrub. Once he almost got caught by several cow hunters but was able to stay concealed even though one of the young men passed within only a few feet. Transfixed on the stranger mesmerized by the way the young man was dressed. When he glanced down at the deer skin shirt he was wearing. No shoes or leggings. Slowly he takes a hold of the bandana around his neck still unsure of its purpose. James admired his skill as he sat confidently atop the large red horse. His heart skipped a beat when the horse turned in his direction stopping short of James' hiding place then quickly sidestepping. He almost stood up and bolted but he stayed hidden and watched relieved as the cow hunter rode away. He wished he could call out to this stranger and sit and talk. He watched as the time of their encounter seemed to pass slowly and was confused because the young man he saw looked just like himself only lighter in complexion. James held tightly to the knife that once belonged to his grandfather. A sick feeling filled his stomach. Not sure what he would have done it he would have been discovered. He feared more his father so he never told him of the encounter. His curiosity was still not satisfied in regards to the white man.

When he returned he pressed his father to tell of why he had abandoned the camp in south Florida. For the life they now lived as mice running and hiding from the approaching white man he could not understand. His father's eyes sharpened as if he was angry at being referred to as mice then he sat next to the fire and stared out into the dwarf cypresses began to speak.

Our people where called by the Spaniards "Cimarrones". We are of the "Hitchiti-speaking tribe", better known as "cow keepers". The boy watches as his father used his hands to tell him, at one time we had herds of cattle that could not be numbered. Life was good and our people roamed from Tallahassee to the north all the way to Okeechobee (big waters) to the south. When the white man came he tried to drive us from the land but we were stubborn and would not give in. My great-grandfather and your mother's great-grandfather fought at the Battle of Wahoo Swamp. For us this was a great battle for the right to live a life we had lived for generations. For the white man it was only for greed. Then they fought the Battle of Lake Okeechobee. James's father now spoke as a proud member of the Seminole people rather than the teacher he wanted to be. He began to give details he had left out when talking of Wahoo Swamp. They moved through the deep saw grass swamp surrounding Lake Okeechobee. Our people used the stiff saw like grass as a deterrent to those who would foolishly follow. As they pushed forward we would have men climbed the tall cypress tree for the purpose of ambush. Here they could fire their guns. There was no way they could move in the thick marsh without our scouts being able to pin point their every move. The mud was deep. He told him again how the large bull disappeared drowning in the deep water. He explained to him regarding the lob-lollies that dotted the marsh. (A lob-lolly is Florida's quicksand, black muck covered with lush green grass that sucked its victims.) The only way we were able to cross was by using the small dugout canoes. The soldiers could not use their horses. Our people were able to kill more of the soldiers than they were able to kill us. We won another great victory that would soon be over shadowed by the cannon exploding over our heads. All they could see were the puffs of smoke followed by thunderous explosions. With one blast they were able to kill whole families. We escaped by heading across Okeechobee driving deeper into the swamp. Many of our people died by snake bite and the alligator, the fever took some of the young leaving families with no one to carry on the traditions of our people.

His father abruptly stands. A hopeless look on his face pointing to the single sickly looking cow feeding just at the edge of the clearing and says, that is all we have now. Pointing toward his mother as she tirelessly labors at the fire and says your mother is all there is left of her family and when I die you will be the only one left to carry on our family. Our people once numbered in the thousands now there are but a few. His demeanor changes as he relaxes and continues. I have met some white men I could trust but they have been very few. He continued by saying I have brought you here because I do not want you to be infected by their greediness and cruel ways. If we can live our lives in hiding and at peace then I will have known I have done my best. Your mother has asked about a wife for you when you get older, I promised her when the time is right we will visit our home in the hammock of our people. Then I will allow you to choose your wife.

James looked bewildered. His father continued. When the time is right you will choose a woman and when you have made your choice we will call the council together making your desires known. A representative of the council will make your desire known to the maiden. After careful consideration and consent is given the process for the wedding begins. At this time your mother and her aunts will deliver gifts of bedding to the family of his purposed bride. The mother of the bride will make you wedding dress. After that a wedding date will be set. At sunset on the appointed day you will go and claim your bride. The next day you along with your new bride will appear together in camp and from that point on you will be considered a couple.

There was a break in his father's voice because he knew when this time came his son would move away and live with his bride's family. With that he turns disappearing into the trail leading to the edge of the lake.

Time passed by slowly for James in this isolated camp. He had explored every inch of the hammock and now was beginning to reach further out into the marsh. This was a fear of his father and he was continually warned not to go too far.

His father watched fretfully as James abandoned his trips into the marsh choosing to stay around camp. A young warrior should run and sharpen his skills in the woods, not lie around camp. One night while James slept his father slipped away from the camp without telling him where he was going. His mother knew and was so excited about the gift they had agreed James needed but promised her husband she would tell him nothing. While on one of their earlier hunting trips on the big scrub they found a small herd of wild horses. James spoke of it often and described in detail the one he wanted and what he would do if he only had a horse. His plan was to capture one for James so he could teach him to ride and the skill of warring. No young Seminole should be without a horse of his own because horses have become such a part of their heritage.

When James awoke he did not see his father questioning his mother as to where he was. All she would say was he had something he needed to do and would be back soon. The next morning James' father had not yet returned. His mother watched nervously the trail he had left on hoping any moment he would return and her fears abated. After answering more questions James's mother finally told him what his father had done. This knowledge only reduced James' fear for a short time.

Hours turned in the days when James told his mother he would try to follow his father's sign before the rain washed it away. He would be careful and bring her word of what he finds. James' mother knew deep down inside her heart her man was dead because that was the only thing that would keep him away as long as it had been. Waves of fear flooded her because it just dawned of the arduous task of finding their way back to their ancestral home. She was angry because he had brought them so far then felt ashamed. She understood his need to preserve his family but why did he have to do it so far from home. Again floods of shame covered her. She reminded herself he was a good father, provider and has taught James many things he will use when he is full grown.

The trail his father had left was at times very difficult for James to follow. In a way he envied his father's skills of concealing his steps hoping to one day to be able to walk across a sand scrub without leaving a single sign of his presence. It did not take long for James to notice buzzards circling high in the sky, swooping down into a small pine island having several tall cabbage trees about a mile to the east. He casually but directly moved toward the pine island holding out hope that it was a dead animal; which drew the buzzards attention. His mind tried to form all scenarios but something deep inside told him the source of the buzzard activity was actually his father.

His greatest fear was realized when he could see a darkened form hanging from the lower branch of a large pine tree. The only thing recognizable as his father was the bright strip of color running down his leggings. He drops to his knees staring in disbelief as his entire life flashes before his eyes. Different emotions swept across his mind like the wind before a strong thunderstorm. Anger, fear, sorrow and rage swell from deep within him but were quickly replaced by concern for his mother. He abandoned his apprehension running toward the swinging form affirming it to be his father. He did not care if anyone was around he cried out questioning why anyone would kill his father for no reason. Overcome by the stench of death but out of respect for his father and the traditions of his people the only thing he could do now was to prepare him for burial. Doubt flooded his mind as if he can remember how to bury him. He thought back to those buried in the hammock where his father had instructed him about traditional burial called, "to-hop-ki" meaning fort. First he took the ax from his bundle and cut two of the straight cabbage trees down. Dragging and rolling them into place he laid them side by side. Cutting smaller saplings he placed the across the two logs and using the rest to make an "X" as rafters and cutting palmetto fans to thatch the roof. Laying his blanket down on the ground he placed his father on it. Pressing red berries he found on the east side of the pine island. Dipping his finger into the red dye he placed a red dot on his father's right cheek. Going to the fire the men who had murdered his father had built picking up a small piece of charred wood he walked back to where his father laid. Touching the end with his finger and places a black dot on the left cheek, then placing the burnt wood in his left hand along with a small bow he had constructed out of respect for his father's memory. In his right hand he placed a single arrow. After he was satisfied with the fact he had faithfully followed tradition. The sun was setting fast. James was extremely tired when he remembered he had not done all he was expected when he gathered firewood as darkness invaded the clearing he built two large fires on either end of the "to-hop-ki". The glow of the fire flooded the small pine island as James turned toward the darkness. His body ached, he felt sick. The stench of death filled his clothes. He had walked as far as he could when he lay down next to a fallen log and fell fast asleep. He only slept for a few minutes before being awaken. James then spent the night close to where he had buried his father knowing his mother would worry but out of respect for his father he would stay. He cried until there were no more tears. Hunger ravaged his body because he had not eaten since leaving camp at daylight. He dismissed the tug on his stomach and sat in silence. His lips burned as the wind blew across his face. Luckily for him the moon was now full. He watched the shadows as they grew from his left than stretching to his right as the moon rose and set. Nature sang a mournful song out of respect for a great man. The cricket set the tone as the hoot owl and whippoorwill sang a doleful solo of reverence for a man they did not know was even alive. His body was now drained of its strength, burning from the many mosquitoes that were stinging his bare arms. He collapsed about an hour before daylight falling into dreams of his happy childhood.

The sun now high in the sky warms his face. The brightness shone through his eyelids awakening him with a start. Gathering what few possessions not taken by the men who murdered his father and wrapping it in the deerskin. Before the small pine island faded in the distance he turned wishing this was all a dream and his father would come around the large palmetto patch next to the tree he was standing next to. James wondered the scrub aimlessly stumbled the entire day. He was no longer hungry. His thirst was satisfied by a small spring bobbling up out of the ground. Finally falling into an uneventful sleep when he finally awoke the sun was setting.

The next morning James returned to the camp. As he entered the clearing his mother knew her husband was dead. Her greatest fear was realized and they are all alone. Even though it was not the Seminole way they stood in the middle of the camp holding each other as James assure his mother everything would be ok.

CHAPTER 20

They spend the night at their camp. James could not sleep so he sat watching as the yellow moon rose in the east. Its dim light flooded the shoreline of the big lake. The eerie sound of the blue heron as it took flight causing him to jump. His heart beat fast as he stares out into the open water. In the silence of the night he could hear bass popping in the lily-pads as they chase unsuspecting minnows. Movement darting from shadow to shadow caught his attention recognizing as a mother raccoon waddled toward him stopping every few feet fishing for crawdads. James sat still wanting to see how close the she coon would come toward him before she realized he was there. Only a few feet away she stops, frozen in her tracks. The raccoon watches this intruder to her world hoping this monster would not see her or harm her litter of babies. Unsure of what she might do James softly spits in her direction. She hisses, turns and makes a hasty retreat still hissing and growling loudly filling the air with her eerie cries literally tripping over her off-spring. The confusion and withdraw of the raccoons made James laugh out loud. His wish was his father could enjoy this moment with him. The reality of his father's absence caused tears to stream down his cheek soaking the front of his tan shirt. It is not the Seminole way to weep for those gone, knowing his emotions would bring more shame than sympathy.

The moon was now high above his head when he decided to return to camp. Retracing his steps back through the thick weeds was surreal. In the distance he could make out the flickering of the fire. Standing in the shadows he could see his mother silhouetted against the darkness as she sat next to the fire. This was unusual for his mother because she went to sleep when the last of the sun streaked across the sky. His heart broke as he witnessed her head buried in her hands. The faint muffled noise as she mourned as Seminole women do, in private was almost more than he could stand. He wanted so bad to rush to her side offering what little comfort he could offer but knew better. James intentionally shuffled his feet so as to not surprise her and as he reappeared in camp she acted as if nothing had ever happened. James smiles slightly knowing her secret was safe with him. She thought he did not notice but before she retired to her bed she wiped her eyes, hugged him and whispered how much she loved him assuring him everything would be ok. James watched in amazement wanting to comfort her and drawing from her strength. He slipped into his bed immediately falling asleep, again dreaming of better days.

James guided the dug out through and around the huge stands of saw grass as if he had done it all his life. His mother watches with pride and comments on how he looked just like his father; which brought a smile to James' face. She orders him to stop as she reaches for the club lying in the bottom of the canoe. Lifting it above her head she brings it down hard onto the surface of the water stunning a large bass lying in the lily pads. He was amazed at his mother's ability as she reaches out flinging the bass into the bottom of the boat. She looks to him telling him they will eat fish when they stop for the night. Continuing on, he missed the turn causing them to head due east. Traveling just a short distance he turns to his mother admitting he may have not turned when he should have. She looks back, both realizing the sun was quickly setting. Before them was a small hammock previously unexplored but would have to suffice for the night. James nosed the dugout no the bank at the same instance a serious of shots rang in the direction they should have gone. James instantly drops to his knees as his mother lies forward hiding her face in the deer skins used as their bed. James could see his mother tremble so they sat in silence hoping not to be discovered. Finally James slips from the canoe making small ripples as he pulls the dugout half way onto the bank. James grabs the spear his father made for him and whispered to his mother to stay hid he would be back for her in just a few minutes. He sticks to the outer edge of the hammock slowly making his way to a natural opening into the thick stand of cabbage trees. He touches one of the trunks lifting his hand. Rolling smut in his fingers evidence of a past fire. Next he ducked under the grapevines that had claimed in and through the few patches of palmettos and sea myrtles. The blade on the spear sliced through the vine as they fell to the side. His heart stopped when he discovered leaning next to a tall cabbage trunk were the remains of someone who had died long ago. Through the torso was lodged a spear resembling the one in his hand. It had strange marking unfamiliar to him, his heart-beat faster as he leant down touching the staff of the spear, running his hand along its length. Squatting down he looked square into the now hollow eye sockets. A shiver of fear and trepidation passed over his body as if someone had touched him. This made him stand stumbling backward readying his self in a defensive stance. At closer examination he could see no indication this was a Seminole, assuming him to be a white man probably deserving this fate. Sharpening his eye he looked around trying to figure out what had happened so long ago. There was no other evidence of a struggle. One thing he could not understand, where is the owner of the spear and why would he leave such a treasure. Taking a firm grip on the shaft of the spear and with one fluid pull dislodged it from the trunk of the cabbage. The dried bones fell into one heap the skull rolled at his feet. He jumped again he shivers, turning hurries further into the hammock making sure it was a safe place to spend a few days. Catching his breath he makes his way back in the direction of the dug-out. When he finally emerges from the thick under growth he could not find his mother. Fearing someone had discovered her and for this reason he did not call out but simple looked for any sign of someone taking her, finding none. All he could find were her foot prints leading in the opposite direction he had first traveled. Noticing several bundles were missing from the canoe he followed the foot prints along the edge of the water. Finally he found her bent over a small spring bubbling up out of coquina rock in the middle of the hammock. She had already cleaned the bass smiling as she told him she was familiar with the island. Assuring him they would be safe for a few days. Her eyes then fixed on the spear in his hand when she nervously asked if she could hold it. Her hands trembled as she stretched them out reverently taking hold of it. Suddenly her eyes open wide recognizing the marking. Deferentially she sets the spear down and steps back with her mouth wide open. Her reaction stunned James stepping over the spear when he heard her screech "no" causing him to side step. Standing now in front of his mother he asked her what was wrong. With this she made him set down and relates to James the spear he found was an important part of their heritage. She went on telling him he must share what he found with the Medicine Man when they finally return to their home camp. James stares at the artifact with amazement, turns toward his mother asking why with his eyes but she simply responded by saying you will have to wait.

Off in the distance they could still hear the sound of gunshot and this lasted until just moments before dark. James gathered small bundles of sticks for their fire and his mother like always prepared a fine meal from meager rations. About an hour after dark James made his way to the south west side of the island and stared out looking across the sea of saw grass. Off in the distance he could see what he believed to be the glow of a camp fire. He was curious wanting to get closer but something inside him told him it would not be a good idea to leave the safety of the hammock. The next night he returned to the same spot and could no longer see the glow determining the threat was no longer there. He returned to the camp telling his mother they would leave the next night.

They loaded the canoe. James pushed the nose of the craft out onto the open water and headed back toward the missed turn. He negotiated the turns with ease making little noise as they headed toward the hammock they camped in before moving to the camp on the lake. They traveled stealth-fully all night enabling them to move across the big scrub by moon light. James was careful not to push his mother too hard but was amazed by her stamina. They stop for a few minutes at a time being careful not to deplete their water supply. They decided to sleep during the day and travel during the night always aware the moon was rapidly waning. Four days later they proudly entered the camp of their family. The one they had originally left almost three years before surprisingly they found it abandoned. James' mother assured him she knew where they had gone. The trip would be difficult through the deep swamp and would take another three days. James watched his mother prepare a hot meal of fresh fish cooked over the open coals and a heaping pot of swamp cabbage. To James it was a meal fit for a chief. He ate every bite with relish. For the first time in many months James was able to sleep without being harassed by his dreams. The next morning both ate what was left over from the night before, dousing the fire they watch as the white smoke ascended through the cabbage canopy disappearing into the brilliantly blue sky.

They were now able to move freely through the swamp following an old trail as it snaked through the cypress trees bigger than those he found next to the clear lake. The path was recognizable to James and his mother because there is a familiarity to the terrine. They could both relax because the trail was only known by their people. His mother was a foot shorter than he and found it difficult to maneuver the deep mud covered by a layer of duckweed. He looked back and watched as the green floating weed concealed their movement giving him a greater sense of calm. At night they would find floating tussocks having to share with water moccasins. The mosquitoes were so thick James could whip handfuls from his face. He could not understand how is mother could sleep so soundly.

At long last they entered the camp and were welcomed by a large group of women who were dressed like his mother. James followed her when she turned to him and told him it was not Seminole tradition for a grown son to follow his mother or be around the women folk. One of the gray headed women pointed toward an open chickee telling him he would find boys his age there. She turns and walks into her aunt's chickee. With a wide smile on her face she commented on how they had not changed since she was a small girl. James turns feeling loneliness for the first time in his life. He never doubted his mother's love but today he was confused as to why she had not told him of this tradition. He notices several young men his age had left the shadows of the chickee and stared as if he did not belong. They laughed and turned running off into the woods. James walks toward the chickee looking curiously at every new sight. He jumped as a white haired man stepped from the darkness and called his name. He was shocked because the voice he heard was that of his father. He turns hoping the last few months had just been a dream, it was not his father. The man introduced himself as his father's brother. James had to look twice because the man looked so much like he remembered his father. They sat talking for hours until the last of the sun light faded away.

They ate heartily on fresh venison and swamp cabbage before being lead to the place he could get a good night's rest.

James was up before day break the next morning. He held in his hand a bundle wrapped in a deer skin. This covering concealed the spear found on the small island in the saw grass marsh. Hesitantly he walks toward the chickee belonging to the Medicine Man. Before he was able to enter the chickee his uncle called to him warning him to not bother the Medicine Man. James insisted he had to see him because he had something he needed to ask him about. At that moment his uncle turned his attention to the package he held in his hands and asked, "Is it about what you hold in your hands?" James looked down holding even tighter on his prize and answered, "Yes". His uncle then pointed toward the opening of the hut telling him to be careful not to bother him too long. Bending over looking into the chickee he could see a slumped from sitting next to the fire. Carefully he entered then stood just outside the reach of the glow of the fire. The old man sat with his back to James when he said. "What is it that you want, James?" This question startled him because he wondered how the old man knew who he was. With his scruff voice he spoke again, "I recognized the step of your father. Where is he?" James moved beside him setting his package down and told him what happened to his father. With passion and reverence the old man spoke of his friendship with his father and how his father would truly be missed. "What is this that you have brought?" turning his attention from the fire to James's eyes. He continued by saying, "You look troubled. What is it, son?" James lifted the package setting it in his lap, gently stroking it. He hesitated before beginning to speak. His glance told volumes to the old man as he stared without comment. He knew nothing he could say would form the words in the young man's mind so with the patience of his many years he waited, stirring the coals of the flickering fire. The old man looked up from what he was doing and began to tell the story of his childhood. He fondly recalls sitting at the feet of man called, Tuc-ma. A Great War Chief of many years ago of which we have been waiting. At the mention of the man Tuc-ma's name James lifted his head and listened with baited breath.

My mother told me to show something to you as soon as we arrived in camp he said as he stood from the stump he was sitting on and handed the bundle to the old man. Gently he un-wrapped the spear then looking at James with his mouth open in awe finally asking. "Where have you found this?" James shared with him what he had rehearsed over and over since his mother told him he needed to show him. The old man listened intently James saw a sparkle in his eye he had not seen before. It was as if he had finally gotten a cool drink of water after being thirsty for days.

The old man stands holding the ancient spear, walked among the camp announcing the need to get out of bed and gather by the fire. Forty-five men, women and children sat next to the fire wiping the sleep from their eyes when the old man announced this was a great day. He turned to James commanding him to tell the story of the spear he now holds over his head. James could hear the gasp as the older population as they recognized the spear and seemed to rejoice at its presence in their camp. James sat confused as he witnessed the reaction of the older people and noticed a wide smile on his mothers face. At that point he knew his mother understood what was happening. Everyone dispersed from the gathering place and busied themselves with preparing a great feast for that afternoon. James was invited into the medicine man's chickee where he was able to finally learn the meaning of the spear.

The old man sat in a semi-circle next to the other elders of the clan. James was given a seat opposite of them as he listened to them talk among themselves. At which point the man sitting next to the Medicine Man stood and handed the spear back to James and said. "Many years ago the Great Spirit spoke to your great-great-great- grandfather Bill Fish and told him that one day a white man would come and take this spear from this place. This broke his heart and tried to hide it. The Great Spirit also told him after it had been gone for many years it would return and the one bearing it would know what we should do. We have grown old waiting for this day to come. That is why today we will celebrate the return of the spear and the one that will show us the way. All this took James by surprise, he tried to question the old men but they were convinced prophesy had come true. Finally they will know what to do.

CHAPTER 21

James sat watching as everyone hurries around preparing for some sort of celebration. He sat in amazement as the old men and women emerged from the numerous structures around the clearing wearing garments from a period long ago. They admired each other's decorative clothing and for the first time since coming here he heard laughter. His mother along with the other women busied themselves with cooking. Sitting in small group they pealed pumpkins, sweet potatoes and wild onions. Some mashed golden kernels of corn in large wooden bowls. The sound reminded James of the sound hogs make as the picked up pieces of corn thrown in the pens as food. Instinctively they moved from one task to another.

He is confused and does not understand why these people would accept him when his father had taken him away from them. He could not accept their way of thinking. He tried hard to compare what his father had taught him to what they were saying as they sat around the fire. He found little difference between the two. The only thing his father said different was that times were changing. He could see it but no one else was willing. A life style that had been a part of their culture for generations will not be viable or sustainable the more the white men came. They had lost the right to own cattle and if they could gather a small herd used only for their survival they were considered cattle thieves and hunted like wild animals. The hammocks in the central part of the state, where they had planted many orange trees and the places held as sacrosanct to their people now are defaced and ravaged by the heartless settlers. As a child he could remember on the large prairies around Thopolacha, once were filled with wild horses they could capture, train and ride without harassment. Now they have but a few horses turned loose by the settlers to die because they are of no use to anyone. If they could capture one if they were caught they would quickly be hung as horse thieves like his own father not but a few weeks before.

His mother noticed James was not with the other young men as they prepared for the hunt. So she went looking for him and found him dumbfounded still sitting next to the fire. As she approached she could see the bewildered look she often saw as a little boy when his father would try to help him to understand the more complex task of daily life. Sitting next to him taking him by the hand she begins to help him to appreciate what is happening. She tells him that this excitement is due to his discovery of the spear, but it was far more that just that. "Our people have lived with very little hope for a long time". She told him as their eyes were fixed on each other, she continued. "This is what your father was trying to do his entire life. He wanted to give them a vision of the future. Fate has fulfilled his dream. He is not here to do this but he is in you, you can help our people. The old men will soon die and the grip of tradition will be loosened, you have been chosen to take your rightful place in this clan. Your great-great-great grandfather was a great chief as was your father's father. Your father's leadership was rejected because he wanted more for his people. Don't have hard feelings for the old men. They foolishly did what they thought best, but now they look for someone to lead them. This task you have been given must not be done allowing pride to rule you. Lead with humility and the spirit of your father, he would be so proud of you."

With that she stood telling him she must go because she was preparing for him a surprise. She also told him to go with the young men and use his skills with the bow and arrow and the spear to hunt the deer. With that she turned James watched as she walked away seeming to float across the clearing. He takes a hold of his father's spear and walks toward the gathering of young men as they prepare to leave the camp, he was greeted by wide smiles of acceptance and welcomed friendship he had longed for his entire life.

That night after James and the others returned. The women dressed the meat and began preparing the meat over the readied coals. He and several of the young men walked down to the creek and swam washing off the sweat, dirt and blood. As they finished James noticed as the young men opened bundles revealing the multi-colored knee length shirts, bright in color. Reds, yellows, dark and light tan. He stared envious wondering where they were able to get such things longing for some of his own. Then the words of his father rang loud in his heart to be satisfied with what you have and hard work will be rewarded. He vowed to himself he would press his mother for some and he would do his part to kill the deer to provide the skin. He smiled as he pulled on a faded pair of tanned knee-high moccasins he had hunted in earlier that day. Now those standing in their bright wardrobe stared at him in shame they had taken such pride in temporal things. As he entered the camp one of the older women ran to him begging him to follow her. Her alarm frightened him as he pushed forward to his mother's chickee. He asked several times what was wrong but she would never answer him as she held a tight hold on his arm pulling him forward. She stopped at the entrance moved behind him giving to him a gentle nudge. With trepidation he pushed through the door and there standing in the dim light of a lightered torch was his mother with a wide smile. He now was irritated because the mystery had frightened him and all he could think about was the possibility of losing his mother as he lost his father. The thought was overwhelming. He eyes narrow as he sharply rebukes his mother for this trick and starts to turn and leave when he saw a suit of the same brightly colored clothes that he had just a few short moments ago were envious of. He looks at his mother and asked without saying a word, how? She smiled at him and told him these once belonged to his father and on many occasions he wore them proudly. She turned toward the other women standing there and said to them as if she was still speaking to her son and said. "He wore them the night we fell in love". Her statement was met with muffled giggles and red faces.

He stood there examining every inch of this finely spun fabric and admired the colors. The turbine fit perfectly as if it was made for him. Atop it stood the white plum of the now vanishing egret, after putting it on he stood for what seemed like hours turning and touching these fine traditional clothing. He was now more confuse than ever because the feeling he now feels cannot be wrong. A pride in who he is and what each piece of this clothing means is such a part of who, he is and who his people are that it cannot be wrong. Standing in the shadows he turns when but for a moment the sun in all its brightness filled the chickee. There standing in the door way is a small humped over figure. He strains his eyes to make out who it was when the he heard the raspy voice of an old women. She steps forward and introduces herself as his grandfather younger sister. She smiles a wide smile turning him about and telling him he looks just like her father when he wore these same clothes. Stunned that these same clothes are as old as she claims but realizes that so many strange things has happened in his life over the past few days that he just accepted her words as truth. She than invites him to sit with her and they talked for hours. When they, at the end of the day emerged from his chickee he at long last realized what his father and the older men were talking about. He came to understand they both were looking for the same thing just in different directions.

The sun was setting as he came from the chickee. It cast its shadows lying long on the clearing. Everything looked different to him. He told this to his aunt and she simply told him they had not changed, he had changed. Taking a deep breath he could smell the cooking meat as the smoke from the fires hover just under the canopy of the towering cabbage trees. They made their way toward the cooking chickee and as they rounded the last hut he was amazed at the gathering of brilliantly color clad people. She chuckled and announced that his cousins have arrived, the Horse and Oak clans.

Every eye fixed upon James as he entered the clearing. Off to one side he noticed the old women chattering among themselves. The children stopped their play and ran toward their mothers hiding behind the ankle length dresses, peering from their hiding place. The old men stood watching as the old women guided him purposefully past the young unmarried women. His attention was immediately drawn to one particular young girl. She was true Seminole with high defined cheek bones. Her evenly tanned body was hard to hide under the vibrantly decorated dress as her hair flows down her back stopping just above her hips. James blushes when their eyes meet, he fears that his looks betrayed him and she knew what he was thinking. He smiles as she simple turns her attention back to the others and began to talk. Aunt Bug knew what she was doing, squeezed his hand and whispered, "She likes you. I will introduce you soon".

James had never gone hungry. His father had always provided for his family but James never saw so much food. Venison grilled over an open fire. Cooked pumpkin, swamp cabbage, fried fish, wild greens and oranges discovered while on the hunt. James talked with the younger men as he retold his discovery of the spear. Assuring each one it could just as well been anyone of them. As he spoke with them he could sense their confidence grow and their allegiance to him get stronger. As the day wore on they played games which drew the attention of the young girls. Each moved from their shaded seclusion onto the edge of the clearing. Their multi-colored dresses fit in a way that called for the young men to take notice. The long black shiny hair caught the reflection of the sun now high in the sky. Each acted as if they were not interested as they watched the young men wrestle. The sweating bodies, trim and well defined glistened in the sunlight. Small clouds of dust lifted from the ground as they tossed each other from one side of the fire pit to the other. A couple of the boys teased James about the prettiest girl that had early shunned his advancement now smiles every time she catches him look her way. Her grandfather was the Medicine Man. She was excited because she had never seen him as energized as he was when he first met this long absent stranger.

James was unaware that one of the other boys liked her before his coming and had warned the others that she belonged to him. He often told of what he would do to anyone he caught trying to get with her. His jealousy could no longer be contained when he rushed forward and tackled him. James, unaware of his words thought at first this advancement was only a playful fight until the other boy drew back his fist and landed a hard strike in the right jaw. This punch addled him almost knocking him out cold. The aggressor turns and looks right at the girl with a devilish smile. James gathers himself and stands to his feet. When the boy turns he realizes he may have made a mistake. James stood taller then he remembered and he stared without expression. He steps toward him now face to face with the boy. James challenges him to a contest for the right to pursue this particular girl. The noise of laughter was replaced by the muffled sound of a confrontation drawing the attention of the elders. They set aside whatever they were doing and joined the now growing crowd. The larger the crowd the more courage the attacker grew. James felt this public challenge was unmerited. Just because this celebration was for him this should not be happening. The challenger's father felt a little embarrassed but knew the ways of his people and would not stop this. James was oblivious to the details of this custom until Aunt Bug stepped up, telling him he must now fight this young man for the right to this girl. His mother stands at the edge of the large crowd when their eyes met. She simple nodded and assured him with a smile. This gave him confidence when he loosened the large knife strapped to his side. The boy opposite him stepped back surprised that he reached for his knife. Custom dictates the man being challenged was the one to pick the weapon to be used in the challenged. A sigh of relief was heard above the chatter of the crowd. James cast his knife aside and stands now ready to face this boy he did not know until this contest.

James outweighed his opponent by twenty pounds and stood almost six inches taller but this did not deter his antagonist. They were reminded of the rules and each was assured this would be a fair fight. They stood opposite of each other and began to circle when James foe took the first swing connecting with James jaw. He had never experienced such pain until the boy realizing he had stunned James and took another swing, than another. He raced in grabbing James around the waist picking him up and driving him into the dirt. This took James breath away and as he scrambled trying to get to his feet he felt the first kick strike his side. Dirt filled his eyes as he was just about to give up when he could hear his father's voice. He told him to remember what he had learned. In his arrogance the smaller boy walked over and began to chide James when he should have finished the fight. All of a sudden James stood rigged. Steadying himself he raised his hands in a defensive posture. When the boy rushed him again, he simple side stepped and delivered a stunning blow to his rival. This angered him to a point he lost his head and went wild. There was murder in his eyes when he reached for his knife setting a top his colorful dress. But before he could react James had his knife out and at the boy's throat. You could hear the gasp for breaths as those watching saw the quickness of James skill with a knife. The boy's father recognized his skill with a knife as that of James' father. Figured this is one area his son could not win so he steps in. The Medicine Man had a feeling this was not over when he steps up raises his hand calling for everyone to be quite. His announcement meant this must end today and it will end by completing a simple challenge. He too had recognized the techniques James used knowing if his father had trained him half of what he knew no one could get close to him with a knife much less cut him. So these are the rules. The first to cut the other is the winner and this will be over. He looked at both boys and spoke to them privately. This is not meant as a chance to kill one another and if it gets to that point I will stop it myself he said. "Do you understand what I am saying". He turns to James and then the boy as they agree to the terms. Each of the boys agreed. They stood opposite of each other then James raised the large knife. The sun shone off of it casting a long shadow.

The circle is reformed as the two opponents square off. Before James could get ready he jumped at the shrill cry and the boy plunges forward as James again side sets bring the knife across the chest of the boy. He stops suddenly dumbfounded as he watches the blood ooze from the shallow cut across his chest. As quickly as it begun it was over and from that day forward James and the boy were friends. This cemented James place in the clan.

JT watched as the old Indian told his story, amazed there was such clarity in his words. There was no hesitation as he told of thing that had happened so many years before. The sun was beginning to set and Henry Lee had not yet returned. In a way JT was glad because he wanted to spend as much time with this stranger to his world as possible. Especially someone he believed came as close to his father as he believed him to. Why did not his father tell him of this encounter and what else about his father did he not know. That night as he lay in his bed roll he dreamed of what it must had been like that day while on the big creek.

The next morning he was awaken by the chattering of a squirrel as it grew irritated by the stubborn seeds hidden deep in the pine cone. JT watched with amusement as in its frustration it would chunk down a resistant cone, falling and hitting every branch as it did. Finally the cone hit with a thud that would cause the squirrel to jump in fear, alarmed. All of a sudden the old man sat up erect having a blank stare. Painstakingly he gathered his belonging packing it securely in the pack he had brought into camp just a day before. JT's heart beat hard because the emotionless movements of the old man. It was as if he was unaware of his actions but his mind far from this place. JT spoke to him but there was no response when suddenly he picked up his spear that JT had admired but too fearful to ask about then headed out into the scrub. It was almost as if he was in some sort of a trance. Quickly JT pulled on his boots picked up the pack the old man had packed but forgot and followed him. JT tried to draw the man out of whatever state he was mentally in but to no avail. He just kept walking. JT thought on several occasions to turn back but his curiosity had now grown so large he could not. About noon they reached the creek swamp. It was as if the old Indian was searching for something. The pace he had started with that morning had begun to wane yet he still held tight to the spear. Every once in a while he would use the end to steady himself but slowly right himself continuing on. JT would rush to his side steadying him but still no response. The sun began to sink in the western sky and the long shadows of the day began to fall when JT realized he was a long way from his own camp and gear. Still holding to the pack and the old man's bow and arrows he realized it would soon be night and he doesn't even have his rifle. He started to turn back when the old man stopped next to a huge cypress tree then collapsed on to the ground in a heap. JT ran to his side turned him to his back so he could look into his eyes. They now where glassed over. JT realized he was dead. Just that quick he was standing there obviously tired from the long day of walking to be dead. JT could not believe it. Now the creek seemed eerie. The katie-did stops it piercing sound, even the rain frog discontinues is plea for rain to honor of the life now gone here on the creek. The mournful coo of the morning dove was more depressing and a flood of emotions washed upon JT. Why would he morn this stranger? Why would he even care if he had died?

Night came faster than normal. JT now sat in total darkness next to a dead man. This was spooky and puzzling to him. He thought of the fire he had left early that morning and all of his gear. He will be lucky if he can even find his camp again or if any of his stuff would be there when he got back. His mind than raced to Henry Lee he was already a day late. Surely he would be at the camp by now and what will he think if he was not there.

JT recalls the means of burial the old man had described in his story and he figured he would try his best to provide this same burial for him. Reaching into his pack he was able to find the means of starting a fire. Soon the darkness was chased to the outer reach of the glow of the fire. The sight of the old man was spine-chilling. He knew as well the night would be long with nothing to shield him from the chill and dampness of the night. He had completely forgotten about his hunger until now. He fumbles around in the old man's satchel finding a few pieces of dried venison; which he ate inhaling rather than tasting. The creek was just steps away from the fire so thirst was not a problem. Off in the distance again he could hear the howl of a lone wolf. Marking the direction and making mental note so he would know the direction to return toward his camp in the morning. So much was happening in his life. The death of his brother, the disappearance of a life he loved dearly, witnessing the last of the wolves that once roamed freely and the death of this Indian. With his death no longer is there a possibility of seeing a free roaming Indian. He thought of the fences he himself had built and the cruelty of men in desperate times. He thought of watching the helpless and stubbornly submissive wild cows as they plunge into the poison solution used for saving their lives. He remembers as they surface with a look of terror on their faces. Gasping and sucking for air swallowing mouthfuls of the toxin facing hours of its affect on their stomachs if it happened to rain too soon after the dipping. All of this seems too much for him to figure out. All he wanted was to get back in the saddle and do what he loved and that was to gather and work cows.

CHAPTER 22

The night felt particularly eerie and for the first time in his life JT was very uneasy in the wilderness he dearly loved. The ancients that James spoke of seemed to visit paying their respect to the passing of an old friend. The night noises were enhanced. The hoot owl sorrowfully announced the coming of another hour closer to another new day. JT longed for the morning.

The smoke from the smoldering fire hung heavy in the air because there was no breeze. It hung within the canopy above his make shift camp. Standing to his feet he hurt all over then looks around seeing the lifeless body of his new friend. Angered that the task of burying the old man was left to him but awed by the reality he was given this responsibility. Throwing a couple of dried pieces of oak he happened to stumble upon the night before. The fire soon blazed high sending forth a welcomed warmth. Reaching into his wallet he took a few pieces of dried beef and ate it with relish. Grabbing his canteen, walked down to the creek, washed his face and filled it. The chore for the day was to gather the Malachierials needed for burying the old man then getting back to camp before Henry Lee and the others returned and find's him missing. Wiping the sleep from his eyes he stumbles as he walks surveying the area. He only walks about one hundred yards when he discovers an already prepared coffin built above ground just as the old Indian had described. He stares in amazement, a wide smile crosses his face knowing now why the old Indian took the time out of his journey and spent this time with him. He needed someone he could trust to bury him the way of the Seminoles people.

JT sat down rehearses all the old man had said and what was expected in the process of burying him. The process seemed difficult but the actual carrying out of the many details was easy. Each piece fit like a puzzle and with little effort but immense respect he placed the last of the logs over the body. After he had lit the last fire and placed all of his belongings on top of the coffin JT realized the big knife was nowhere to be found. He carefully retraced his steps back to the place where he fallen and died but it was nowhere to be found. An unexplained anxiety engulfed him, like as always he spoke to himself. A way of figuring things out by talking to his self into something he really does not want to do. Did he have it with him or did he pack it away in his pack he left back at the other camp? Aware he could not stay here any longer he abandoned his search and headed back toward his camp, retracing carefully each step. He had walked for several hours when he saw the riders emerge from the oak hammock and stop. He eases behind a tree because he felt vulnerable without his rifle or knife. The spears seemed useless but it brought some comfort. There were three riders and four horses. He was extremely relieved when he recognized it to be Henry Lee bring him a horse. He knew he would be considered a little touched in the head until he would be able to tell them the story, yet he was use to be treated this way. Satisfied only in the knowledge that he knew truly how they felt about him.

The first to see JT as they entered the scrub was Will Magrit he turned toward him and trotted his way closely followed by the others. JT looked weary and tired but glad to see them. Finding some shade they stopped for the noon meal which JT ate as if he had not eaten in days. He told them of his visitor, of following him in the darkness and then burying him on the creek. They rode back to the place he had slept and JT showed them the place of his burial and asked if this place could be kept secret; to which all agreed. All rode along hanging on every word JT spoke while deep down inside each wished they too would have had the experience he had.

While on their way back to the Magrit place they happened upon a bunch of cows that looked to be due a dipping. Each of the men with a keen eye looked around and saw no one. Instinctively they circled the cows and began to move them slowly toward the closest dipping vat located at Cow Pen Branch when the first shot was heard and the alarming sound of a bullet passing close to Henry Lee's head. The three old men with lightening speed spun around sitting atop their horses with rifles drawn as the next bullet struck the horse JT was riding. The horse bucked violently throwing JT hard onto the ground. The horse toppled over pinning him under its side. Henry Lee maneuver his horse to one side while Jibby goes the opposite direction all the time sending volleys of shot in the direction of the attacker. JT lay under the horse cursing the pain he felt in his leg struggling hard to free his lodged rifle but to no avail. Will Magrit, without thought took a more direct route straight in the direction of the sniper. It was over as soon as it begun with the capture of a single man who was under the impression the entire time his cows were being stolen. Henry Lee Tanner had a sharp and explosive temper and it was now raging. He wanted to whip the man and would have if it had not been for JT still being pinned under his horse hollering for attention. After freeing JT from under the horse Henry Lee began teasing him about having to give him a dog fennel to ride, at least he could not kill that.

Jibby called for the foolishness to stop because they needed to deal with this stranger. If he had been a better shot he could have killed anyone of them. Not knowing when to keep his mouth shut, the stranger spoke up saying he hit what he was shooting at. His boastful comment was met with Henry Lee right hand. The hit was so hard it echoed off the towering pines and thick palmettos. To every one's surprise the man was back on his feet and back in Henry Lee's face. This time before anyone could say a word he had hit Henry Lee several time with a quickness none had ever seen. The strikes addled Henry Lee causing him to stumble backward but he never lost his footing. Both JT and Will looked confused at Jibby wondering why he did not help his brother but their concern was soon answered when Henry Lee straightened himself and threw the next punch. His fist hit with such a resounding thud the result was the stranger melting into a single heap on the ground, out cold. Jibby then smiled at Henry Lee and said. "He kicks like a mule and caught me by surprise when he hit me". Henry Lee rubbed his jaw, bent down and picked up his hat placing it back on his head then said. "We ought ta leave him there for the ants to get but let's wake him and see what's his story". Henry Lee poured some water on him he woke slowly disoriented and confused. He stood then walked over to Henry Lee with his hand extended. Henry Lee did not know what he was doing so he took a defensive stance drawing back his right hand. The man raised his hands in front of him indicating he was no longer a threat telling

Henry Lee all he wanted to do was shake the hand of the first man ever to knock him out. He thought he was arrogant and did not like the man. He turned and ignored him for as long as he could when Jibby turned telling him next time he thought he could come into another man place and want to fight, he better think twice. With that Henry Lee climbed back into the saddle the silence only broken by the creaking of the long whip as he got the small bunch of cows moving.

CHAPTER 23

Again JT found himself a foot but this time it was not his fault. It was suggested he find another place of camp and they would again be back in a few days. He adamantly said no and assured everyone he would carry his saddle and gear all the way back to Christmas if need be but he was not spending another night alone out in the scrub. He told them he was tired and hungry. Henry Lee spoke up and said. "Why didn't you tell me you was hungry. I got some extra fried sweet potatoes you can have." JT looked at him just shaking his head in disbelief. The man who had shot JT's horse spoke up telling them he had several head of good horses back at his camp a mile to the west offering to give JT one if they would just let him go. Henry Lee shifted in his saddle looked right into the eyes of the assailant and said. "How can we be sure these are your cows and horses? You could have stolen them and just getting rid of a problem." The man smiled assuring him all the animals belong to him mentioning he had purchased them from a man by the name of Rabbit Roberts. After hearing the name Roberts everyone seemed to relax agreeing to take the horse if he would ride along to Cow Pen Branch because Will insisted the cows were going to be dipped whether he liked it or not. He explained to him he had a tick free herd not too far from where they were standing and he aimed to have them remain that way. Tightening his legs against the side of his horse he moves close to the stranger extends his hand and introduces his self. "The names, Hatcher, Slim Hatcher and I's from south Georgia around Blackshear." Will's next question was what made him come here in particular. Slim told him he had lost his family to the fever and was run out. So he packed what little he had and headed south. He had spent a few years over on the east coast but got tired of the mosquitoes and yellow flies and had to find some relief. He turned and shown a mouth full of black half broken teeth. The teeth in his mouth were so rotten that every time he opened his mouth you could smell pure rot. Henry Lee commented the smell would gag a buzzard off a gut wagon but his joke soon got old and tiresome. As they rode and talked he would reach into his wallet and take a swig of moonshine to which he said helped with the pain. This practice irritated Will because he could not tolerate a man wasting his time or money on such foolishness. Henry Lee had as much of the stink as he could handle when he suggested the man to go to Kissimmee and see the new dentist maybe he could help him. Henry Lee added. "You got to make yer'self sick haven to smell yourself, see'ne your nose is so close to your mouth." To this everyone laughed, even Will who was always so serious.

Will told him he had just purchased some young colts from a man up north and they needed breaking. He agreed to give one to JT if he was interested in breaking two for him to ride. JT promised to begin first thing the next morning; that is if he actually makes it home this time.

As they came to the last rise in the scrub just before entering the creek swamp at Cow Pen Branch they could hear the presence of another herd being dipped at the vat. The lowing of cows and the men yelling sounded like there was a lot of confusion. Will and Jibby looked at each other baffled by the commotion. They themselves had assisted in dipping everyone's cows just a week ago and they knew they were not due for another week.

Jibby motioned for everyone to stop telling Slim Hatcher to stay with his bunch of cows while they rode ahead to determine who it could be. Before Will rode off following Jibby he assured Slim that he did not want his cows mixed with anyone else if they were infected.

Henry Lee believed it to be some of the Partin's because when they worked cows they were always loud but he was unsure. Thinking nothing about it they pushed their horses through the waist deep dark water then up the steep bank onto the other side when all of a sudden they were confronted by three young men on horseback pointing repeater rifles right in their face. This startled Will and JT but aggravated the Tanner brothers because these strangers are not from around here and they are using a vat they did not help build. For no apparent reason these men stand now in their way. On top of that they had the nerve to point their rifles in their chest. Henry Lee feared no man but respected someone having a gun shoved into his chest. Will stepped up taking a hold of the situation first asking what outfit was using the vat. The young man standing closest to

Henry Lee said sarcastically they were the Sander's from west of Apopka. A fire swept through and destroyed their pasture and they were about to lose the herd. He continued by saying they were not going to be here long. Their plans were to turn north once they reached the river making a big circle back home before Christmas time. The reason they were using the vat was because some crazy old man by the name of Will Tanner told them if they were going to range their herd around this area they would have to dip the cows or he would have to gather men and by order of the United States Department of Agriculture they would kill the entire herd. He went on to say. "I guess pa believed him cause that's what we's doing. I think it's all bull…." Before he finished he called Will a name, a name I just wouldn't repeat but it brought the swift retribution in the form of a right hand from Henry Lee right across the mouth. It sent the young man sailing off his horse landing flat of his back out cold. His quickness startled the others causing them to coward while still pointing their guns now solely on Henry Lee. He could tell they were scared and a scared man with a shaky finger. A loaded gun and a scared man was not a good combination. He looked straight in their eyes and said. "If you don't want the same I would put down them guns and follow me to the pens. By the way when he wakes up tell him no one talks about my brother like that without tooting an ass whippen." Jibby moved his horse over the boy lying on the ground making his big black stud horse step over him like he was not even there. Henry Lee simply smiled and tipped his hat as he too stepped over the boy now slowly recovering. As JT passed he looked down and seen the expression of bewilderment and confusion plastered all over his face topped off by a swollen black eye. They all made their way toward the pens when they were met by a tall slender man atop a slick black mule. Sweat poured from his brow and his shirt was sopping wet. He coughed constantly and cussed the smell of the arsenic complaining about having to constantly drive his cows from one vat to another. To his belief it was a waste of time and had never seen one cow sick from the tick fever.

Immediately Bill Sanders recognized Jibby and extended his hand in greeting. The two men had been long time acquaintances but never close friends. After the two men said their hello's the father of two of the young men who greeted Jibby and his party at the creek noticed his son coming toward him stumbling holding his right eye. Before anyone could say a word Bill Sanders stepped from his horse and grabbed the boy by the collar insisting persistently as to who was responsible for this. Shaking him violently he finally pointed to Henry Lee and said. "That old bastard over there with the big black hat." Bill turned and realized it was Henry Lee he was speaking of. Turning back to the boy and struck him with the back of his hand with such force the boy rolled across the ground dumbfounded as to why his father would treat him this way in front of strangers. Shaking his head he climbs back in the saddle, driving his long spurs into the side of his horse causing it to lunge forward pressing up against Henry Lee's horse and asked why he felt it necessary to hit the boy as he did. Henry Lee matched his pressure as his big black stud set his feet and leaned against the much smaller horse and looked right into his eyes and told him what happened. He relaxed turned in agreement with Henry Lee's form of justice. They rode back toward the vat where the progress in dipping the cattle had stopped as those with the Sander's stopped and watched the excitement. Bill explained as to why they were here and he assured Jibby and the others as soon as they were through here they were heading back toward home. He told them they knew how to deal with the Ranger Riders over in their neck of the woods. This comment angered Will Magrit because he had heard about several men being killed in a gun battle over that way only a few weeks before. Will told him it would be a good idea for them to finish and leave as soon as possible because they were going to follow the law as long as they are east of Orlando. Will felt no threat and meant none but Bill did and challenged him to which Will stepped down from his horse right into the face of the aggressor. A mistake he will never make again. Bill hit him in the jaw which caused him to loss his balance but he quickly righted himself and flew into him and when all was said and done Bill stood leaning against a large pine breathing hard. Blood rolling from an open cut above his eye and he said. "Ya'll got too short of a temper. I was just fun'nen but I know when I been beat." The mood had softened and after the last cow was driven through the vat the four strangers from west of Orlando turned back west and headed home. Jibby, Will, Henry Lee and Ben rode east toward Christmas and Will and JT headed north east toward the Magrit place. They talked little about the day's activities really never saying anything other than saying they hoped for the day when there will be an easier time.

Early the next morning JT woke before daylight and made sure his saddle was fit for breaking the horses. In the large pen behind the barn were five of the prettiest young horses he had ever seen. Instantly he fell in love with the bald face gelding. After breakfast he gathered his gear and made his way back to the pen. Taking his long stiff rope he tossed it over the head of the gelding and it instantaneously became tight. JT was in a battle against this young horse

August 1922

The sun was high and hot in the sky. JT rode across a scrub somewhere north of Paine's Prairie. After leaving Will Magrit he hired on as a Ranger Rider and was assigned north Florida. At the time of his hire he was only one of two hundred riders that covered the entire state and watched thirty two hundred known dipping vats. During the hay day of the cattle boom in Florida families moved all across the state in search of better pasture for their cows. Most lived a nomadic lifestyle having their original homestead and then having a secondary home to the south. When the cattle market was closed in the Keys and Havana and the need for beef further north was open to western beef some families sold their herds to larger cattlemen and faded back into a life style of farming and other enterprise. Families by the name of Slaughter, Smith, Bass, Townsend, Sanders, Osteen and Vaughan once were linked with the cattle business but no longer. They adapted to the times and many made money as most Florida families could do in producing tobacco, watermelon, peanuts and sweet potatoes. While others moved close to the west coast and fished. There was even a family that started producing char-coal.

JT rode up to the only known vat in Alachua County and the area bustled with activity. This was JT's first assignment. Not knowing anyone in the area he asked around trying to determine who was in charge. He introduced himself and identified himself to a young man by the name of Poley Horne. They were busy pushing the cattle along as fast as possible because the storm clouds were gathering to the east and the smell of rain hung heavy in the air. JT stands back and watches as the last few cows plunge into the arsenic solution. The second to jump went under the water as the others plunged in on top of her and before they could get the bunch untangled the cow drowned. JT not being one to stand back leant a hand and grabbed one of the ropes around the back legs. While standing on the edge of the slippery vat JT's foot slipped along with a young man and both went head long into the vat right next to the dead cow. As soon as he hit JT was back on the edge of vat. He knew what could happen to someone who swallowed this toxic solution. The young man was too weak to move as fast as JT due to the fact he had just started getting over the last time he fell in and almost died. JT reached out for the terrified young man, his mouth open trying to say something when the dead cow rolled because of the commotion in the six foot deep vat washing the toxin into his mouth. He coughed and spit trying to remove the liquid from his mouth but it was too late. He went into convulsions with white foam erupting from his open mouth and slipped under the surface of the water. Poley jumped into the water careful to not let his head sink beneath the surface and lifted the lifeless body of the young man. The boy's father leap from his horse and ran to his side. The pain on his face told the story of his grief as he shakes his dead son violently to no avail. JT steps back and asked where the closest source of clean water. Walking to his wallet that hung on the horn of his saddle, retrieving a bar of lye soap and quickly took off his drenched clothes casting them to the side then he dove underneath the cool spring water. The shock of the cold caused him to drop the soap forcing him to go after it as it was pushed along by a rather stern current. He washed as fast as possible then climbing out standing in the heat of the day freezing. His teeth chattered as he dried himself as good as possible and pulled on his extra pair of britches. Bending forward he unfolds his shirt then turned and there standing right in front of him was the prettiest red headed girl he had ever seen. Immediately his face flushed red. He was embarrassed because he could not have had his pants on when she first walked up. He feared she saw him naked and that was just not right.

She stands before him with a wide smile on her face and asked for his wet clothes so she can wash them for him. Awkwardly he hands her the tight bundle of dripping clothes and he watches dumbfounded as she scurries of. He later learned that her name was Molly and the sister of Poley. By the time he had returned the body of the dead boy was loaded in the back of an old Model T and it was just pulling away. Poley and Molly rode up next to where JT was standing and they asked if he had a place to stay while in the area. His response was no, and then they invited him to follow them home and stay with them. Molly told him it was her father's idea because of his help to try and save their brother. Strangely there were no tears or any sign of grief in the expression of either the boy or the girl. They rode across a black jack oak scrub toward their home near a small community on the Suwannee River.

JT spent a week in the same area always finding his way back to Osteen home every night. He thought that he would never find someone like Molly and believed he was falling in love. The night before he was to leave and return to the big creek he asked Molly who was only seventeen if she would go with him and be his bride. He had no idea she would say yes but to his surprise she jumped into his arms and shouted yes. All the commotion brought her parents to the front porch and her father did not like the fact that JT held her so close. She told them of her intentions and with relief on her mother's face she announced that the wedding will be Saturday. The suddenness of news scared JT to death. He tried to back away from the wedding being so soon but Molly would not allow it, so JT is getting married on Saturday.

That night it begun to rain and it rained hard for the next three days. On the morning of the wedding the sun rose and the sky was clear. The river flooded and the brown water filled every creek and pond all around the Osteen home. This did not hamper the celebration and as planned the wedding happened right on time. The gathered family and friends danced, eat their full and the men took short nips on the free flow of moonshine. About an hour before dark Molly came to JT and told him she believed it time to get started. Her father had given them an old wagon to which JT hitched the old mare Molly was riding the first time they met. He threw his saddle in the back of the wagon along with all that belonged to Molly along with tying his horse to the back and off they went. The moon was high and almost full. The light flooded the scrub illuminating the deep rutted dirt trail leading south east. JT's heart beat loud the further they traveled away from her home. Finally they stopped and JT built a fire while Molly prepared the back of the wagon for a safe place to sleep. As he returned to the wagon she stops him and kisses him inviting him to join her in the back of the wagon. JT experienced something that night he had never known and his love for Molly was cemented forever.

The next morning the sky was over cast and there was a threat of rain. JT wanted to get as far as possible before night fall but the old wagon caused them to have to move slowly. They decided to abandon the wagon if they cannot sell it at the next settlement they come to. Finally they were able to leave behind the wagon and climb on horseback and quicken their pace toward Christmas. The first night beyond the leaving the wagon a strong storm blew in from the south and JT nor Molly had never witnessed such rain. The lighting struck all around them and the compression of the rumbling of the thunder would not allow them to sleep. JT holds Molly close to him. He could feel her tremble and jump with a start at every strike. Within thirty minutes of the first drop of rain until two hours after daylight they were soaked to the bone.

The wood around the small scrub they camped at was wet and it made it difficult to start a fire so JT could help Molly to get warm. Because of sheer exhaustion Molly ultimately feel asleep and lay shivering. About noon she awakens drenched with sweat. He tried everything to break the fever than in frustration sat next to her and just stared at her as she slipped away. He felt helpless as he tried desperately but to no benefit. At four in the afternoon she took her last breath. He had lost his mother and father. He had lost his best friend and brother. But the emotions that surfaced due to the loss of Molly could not be compared. He hurt an awful lot.

The sun was setting, the days were getting shorter. He sat next to her wondering just how much he was going to be asked to bear. Should he try and take her back to her parents or should he just bury her here say his good-byes and ride on.

That night while sitting next to the fire he remembers the old Indian and the way he wanted to be buried. The night was filled with noises that seemed to be louder than before. He decided to not return to north Florida. The next morning he used the small spade to dig a hole and gently placed his wife in. After the last shovel of dirt was placed over her body he saddled his horse, dallied off Molly's horse behind his and headed south. He rode aimlessly for days only stopping long enough to sleep and eat. One week to the day Molly passed away dismounted his horse in front of the Magrit place. Will was not at home probably out riding through his cows a practice he enjoyed doing. Tying the horse to the front rail JT crawled up on the front porch and went to sleep.

Will came home about an hour later and noticed him a sleep and decided to allow him to remain a sleep he figured because he was a sleep he must truly be tired. JT woke about an hour before dark noticing his horses were moved. Rubbing his eyes JT watched him emerge from the barn carrying a bucket. He acknowledged JT as he passed on his way to feed the hogs.

That night at supper JT told of his experience with the small boy that drowned in the dipping vat. He was sickened by the whole incident and could not believe how fast the poison could kill. During their conversation he casually mentioned his marriage to Molly Osteen. Will set his coffee cup down and just stared at JT in disbelief. Not that he had gotten married, because he himself had done the same thing when he met a pretty little thing. He was troubled by the nonchalant and indifferent attitude of someone who had just lost his wife. This attitude concerned Will and he meant to speak to him but never got the chance.

CHAPTER 24

One night JT sat in the glow of the oil lamp and thought back to the day he met his wife. A broad smile crossed his face as he reminisced falling into a deep dream filled night.

He was startled awake by the sound of a wagon stopping just outside the front of the door of the barn. Instinctively he reached for his rifle easing toward the door so he could get a look at who would come uninvited to his home so early in the morning. To his surprise, the first person he saw was Sarah. Others were milling around the clearing, finally he emerged from the barn still wearing the same clothes from the day before. Sarah saw him coming from the barn, raced toward him throwing her arms around him almost knocking him to the ground. She took a step backward and said, "I am so sorry." JT was puzzled by her words, gently pushed her away while looking at her mother Aunt Kittie. Her father was also standing not far from them. Aunt Kittie spoke up, being a women that spoke her mind and told JT they were concerned for him after hearing about what had happened the night before and asked if the family could visit for a while. She said jokingly they maybe fish in the creek. "It would be fun to have a fish fry". She said while busying herself with unloading her cane poles. JT told them of a deep hole to the south. He spoke as he saddled his horse. They could go and see if the fish were biting. Sarah turned to her father and asked if she could ride a horse with JT. He said with irritation in his voice she should have thought about that earlier because he didn't have a horse in his pocket. JT spoke up and said she could ride his old horse because he wanted to ride the young filly to see how she would do out on the scrub. Her father spit a long stream of brown juice agreeing with a smile.

Sarah ran from the wagon carrying a brown package to the front porch disappeared into the house. JT looked at everyone confused shrugging his shoulders. The expression on his face was as if she had lost her mind when Uncle Homer simple said, "women". JT quickly turns and heads to catch the horse when he heard the familiar sound of the front door opening. He turned to see Sarah standing on the front porch wearing an altered pair of her brother's britches revealing Sarah to truly be a woman. Still grabbing for the horse he could not take his eyes off of her. As she passed him she smiled knowing she had now gotten his undivided attention. JT really liked what he saw and could not wait to get her alone at the creek so he could tell her how pretty she was. She slowly walked to the wagon placing the rolled up dress into the bottom of the wagon. She again walked past JT entering the barn and like a puppy unaware of his actions JT quickly followed. She grabbed for the saddle, he asked if she needed help she said. "I might need some later", smiling a wide grin spread across her face. She guaranteed his she had everything under control. After getting the saddle on the back of the large horse, she flirtatiously called for JT to show her how to cinch it even though she was an accomplished horsewoman. Her father started to say something about the many times she had saddle her own horse when she gave her father the same look her mother did when he had said too much. He turned aggravated leaving the barn before JT saw the annoyance on his face. He walked up behind her while reaching around her to show her how it was done he became intoxicated by the smell of lavender in her hair. She turned finding them face to face. Immediately his thoughts were racing and at this moment he faced the most feared creature on earth, a woman who was so fascinating but worth watching out for. Their eyes met looking deep into each other's eyes. He was trapped. JT drew Sarah close to him and kissed her. Forgetting her family was there, he could not let her go. Aunt Kittie entered the barn just as he withdrew from her embrace when she turned with a wide smile on her face softly clapping her hand in approval of this relationship. She knew this was improper but if her only daughter were going to find a suitable husband she would have to be a little forward. This is not acceptable but sometime necessary. Sarah was now nineteen and had shown little interest in any of the young men that had come, calling. She had only spoken of JT assuring her mother if he were to ask her to marry today she would without hesitation.

CHAPTER 25

They walked from the barn leading the horses. Sarah wore a broad smile on her face and the sun had never been as bright. For the first time in a long time, since she was a little girl had she heard so many birds sing so loudly. Life to her was perfect. JT was immediately brought back to reality when he noticed the entire family standing staring watching with more teeth showing then he had ever seen. His face flushes red, embarrassed by their possible knowledge of his thoughts and actions in the barn and afraid of how Uncle Homer would react because his conversation while on the hunt was still very fresh in his mind. To his surprise no one said a thing when all of a sudden Aunt Kittie hollered bringing everyone back to reality announcing she was now ready to go fishing.

JT gently lifted Sarah into the saddle of the tall horse then he sprang onto the back of his young filly. His quick action caused the young horse to spin and crow hope to one side. The small horse spun nervously in a circle but it did not take long for Will to bring her under control. He led the Partin's across the clearing then out into the scrub. The clanking of the trace chains set a rhythmic beat as the mules stumbled along. The sides of the wide wagon scrapped and brushed through the palmettos adding to the thrashing and swishing of the mule's tails. The buck knot plant filled the ride with a strong sweet aroma. Aunt Kittie could not stop talking the entire ride as they bounced along following JT and Sarah down the wash out leading to the ford across the creek. The massive oak trees combined with the blooming bay trees interlaced with cabbage trees towering sixty feet in the air provided a peaceful shade. The smell of fish chased the sweet smell rapidly away filling the air only adding to the excitement as they drew up in a grassy clearing on the other side of the creek. The wagon had not completely stopped when Aunt Kittie demanded one of her sons help her to the ground. She impatiently stomped her foot demanding help. With a bucket of worms in one hand and two long cane poles in the other she became more impatient by the minute. Her oldest son lifted her from the back of the wagon. Everyone laughed because her feet were kicking in anticipation and as her feet hit the ground she was off in the direction of the creek. She had not taken too many steps before walking right into a large spider web still occupied by a huge banana spider. In survival mode Aunt Kittie flung the worms in one direction and the pole in another, as she danced literally bouncing off of the cabbage trees along the path trying hard to free herself from the grasp of the web and the spider who was trying as hard to get away. Her squeals echoed in the canopy of tall trees causing a woodcock to take flight sending forth an alarm and the whistling of its wings of some strange intruder into his world. Uncle Homer laughed out loud and danced a gig flinging his arms mocking Aunt Kittie. His actions drew immediate laughter from the children but a stern glare from the heavy breathing Aunt Kittie followed by a few hours of silence. It did not bother Uncle Homer much until it came time for frying the fish. Aunt Kittie refused to do her part. Everyone now knew for sure that she did not like to be made fun of and there was a cost to, "playing the fool" as she called it.

After the ruckus with the spider JT and Sarah slipped off by themselves and found a sharp bend in the creek creating a deep swirling hole. Last spring he caught several large catfish in this hole knowing if they were patient they too could have the same luck. Sarah sat down and pulled off her boots. Than settling down on the white sandy banks, working her toes into the warm sand teasing JT until he relented and followed suit. They sat without saying a word when all of a sudden they heard Aunt Kittie squeal announcing to anyone near and far she had caught another fish. Sarah laughed; which broke the awkwardness of their silence. JT fumbled with his words as he complimented her on her beauty and her aggravation. Sitting next to him with her knees pulled up to her chest toes still working in the sand she smile, blushes as she scoots closer to him. Her touch does something strange to him and instantaneously he felt guilty. He could not understand how he felt. He thought of running finding a place where he could think about what is going on and not Sarah. JT had not been unsure of himself since he was on his first trip to cow camp but today he felt foolish and wanted to just react without thinking. He did not like this feeling. They sit for a few more moments when Sarah finally spoke. She asked if he had ever thought about getting married and if he had what kind of girl was he looking for. Her forwardness surprised him when in reality it scared him to death because he was not use to being in the company of a female especially one he really liked. Suddenly the bobber began to dance on the surface of the creek then disappeared under the surface of the swift running dark water. Impulse took over Sarah pushed JT aside as she grabbed the pole straining as she hoisted the catfish to the surface. It rolled over and over as she drug it toward the shore. It flopped and splashed at the edge of the water still securely hooked trying desperately to shake itself free. JT using his foot kicked the fish further up the bank as Sarah drops the pole and grabs for the fish when it finned her in the palm of her hand drawing blood. The pain was intense and quickly swelled. JT takes his chewing tobacco from his back pocket placing it in his mouth swirling it, getting it wet then putting it on the area the catfish struck. The tobacco drew the poison from the wound as the pain subsided. He blushes again when he realizes he was holding her hand. Sarah smiled at how awkward he acted when she grabs his chewing tobacco putting some in her mouth. She smiled a big smile, turned walking toward her catfish and bounces off toward the fish. JT was so confused by Sarah's actions. One minute she is so shy and acts as a little girl unsure of herself than the next she was impetuous. He really likes her self-confidence but there is something about her manner he finds strange. Reaching in the bucket she retrieved another craw-dad hooking it behind the head and tossing it out into the middle of the creek. She reminds him of her question of which he had not forgotten but tried to dismiss it. They settled back down and finally he is able to answer her question. Cautiously he tells her he had always thought about one day marrying and having a family but he was not sure this was in his present future. Before he could finish Sarah climbs to her knees and throws her arms around his neck kissing him on the cheek. Instantly he dismissed his indecision and melt in her arms. The bobber disappears without their attention as the pole slowly slips into the dark water. Finally she releases him allowing him to take a deep breath. His mind floods with thoughts of Sarah and how wonderful it would be to be married to her. She fishes, rides a horse by straddling it, hunts and can cook. She is the perfect woman, so why is he so reluctant.

Again she sees her pole disappearing as she jumps to her feet grabbing the pole. She does a little gig looking just like her mother, as she pulls another good size catfish to the bank. This time she needed no help in landing the fish and smiles at JT as she puts her thumb in his mouth removing the hook. He shakes his head because he cannot figure her out. One minute she is helpless then independent, needing no one. One minute she throws herself at him the next she acts as if they are just strangers fishing. He whines the fishing string around the pole then picks up the two fish hanging on a fresh palmetto fan and walks back toward the day camp. Uncle Homer was cleaning their fish and placing a Dutch-oven above the fire so the lard can get hot enough to fry the fish crispy. Every once in a while everyone can hear Aunt Kittie hooping and hollering in concert with each fish she pulls from the deep dark water. Uncle Homer suggested they spend the night and it was decided to camp for the night. JT did not come prepared so he had to head back to his place in order to feed up and get his bed roll. Sarah asked if she could go. JT did not think this would be a good idea because he did not know if he could trust himself with her alone. She dismissed his apprehension and quickly saddled her horse. Climbed up on the horse and would not take no as an answer.

They rode for a few minutes before Sarah kicked the horse she was riding in the flank causing it to lurch forward. Her action startled JT and he followed suit. He watched as she bounced and enjoyed seeing her hair blow in the wind. Over the bridge and into the front yard she slips from the saddle and rushes toward the back porch. JT had all but become convinced that women are crazy as he followed her to the back porch. To his shock he caught a glimpse of her naked body flying through the air disappearing below the surface of the water. His heart skipped a beat trying hard to process what he had just seen. She comes up laughing out loud and calls for JT to join her when he turns and heads for the barn to do his chores. The entire distance he argued with his good nature that it would not hurt to joining her but he feared her advances more.

She became ashamed by her forwardness hoping she did not do anything that would drive him away. She climbs to the back porch quickly dries off and dresses. She blushes as she approaches him apologizing for her actions asking if he liked her or not. JT assured her he does but her actions scares him and he did not trust himself seeing her as he did on the back porch. She smiles telling him he would do nothing to her or with her that she did not want him to. She admitted her love for him and says as she turns and walks away. "I ani't gonna wait much longer." and disappears around the large palmetto patch heading back toward camp. He finishes his chores and sits dumbfounded on the edge of the porch wishing

Mr. Magrit or someone were here so he could ask them about what was happening inside.

The fire glows casting it light upon the tall trees along the creek. The amber sparks float upward disappearing into the darkness. The hoot of the owl caused memories to flood his mind thinking back to the first time he and Lize camp here. He smiled and wishes he could return to those simpler days. Aunt Kittie was already asleep in the back of the wagon. She snored so loud Uncle Homer said she rattled the wagon. JT sees an inviting figure step down from the wagon and stand just on the edge of the light the fire cast, then disappearing into the darkness. Her hope was JT would follow her but he did not. Taking his bed roll he shook it out and lay down beside the fire. Even though the ground was hard it was sleeping out under the stars he felt the most a live and satisfied. He lay on his back looking through the trees above his head watching the stars. The frogs along the bank of the creek crocking in concert were the last thing he hears.

Early the next morning JT was awakened by the sound of clanking pans as Aunt Kittie prepared breakfast. The smell of fresh biscuits filled the camp as he rolls on his side watching as she moved methodically around the fire still the only true source of light. He rolls over on his back and is startled by the fact that Sarah was sound asleep next to him. He jumps up grabbing his boots because he did not want anyone to think anything had happened. Her forwardness irritated him and he knew he had to have some time to figure out what he was feeling. He knew something was happening and he knew he was falling in love with her but the suddenness of it all sacred him. This confused him even more because he did not fear anything. He has had to kill men before and have faced some difficult situations. He has faced down many an angry bull and wiry rank cow but this nineteen year old female terrified him the most.

After pulling on his boots he walked to where he had hobbled his horse taking the brush from his wallet and brushed her down. He felt comfortable around his horse and tired hard to separate his feelings but was unsuccessful. Finally coming to a decision he walked to the fire and sat patiently for the sun to rise. He helped Aunt Kittie lift the heavy cast iron kettle from the back of the wagon setting it next to the fire. He sat without saying a word until finally she sat next to him assuring him she understood what he was feeling and if he needed some time to work things out she would talk to Sarah. One thing she asked was not to drag this out because Sarah deserved to know soon, to which Will agreed. She stood wrapped a few hot biscuit and fish in a brown piece of paper, handed it to him telling him to leave before she woke up. She assured him she will take care of everything. With those few words he had never experienced so much relief when he rode out onto the scrub just as the sun broke the horizon.

He never stopped at his place just continued to the Magrit place. The further he rode from where they had camped the more he wanted to turn around and head back so he could be there when she woke up. But he knew he needed to talk to someone who could help him separate this all out and understand it. He had never needed anyone before so this was all new to him.

CHAPTER 26

JT rode lazily through the scrub noticing thing he before times had not seen. The birds seem to sing a lot louder. The sun shone brighter and the breeze a lot cooler. He thought he was going crazy. Within an hour he entered into the clearing at the Magrit place and was greeted by Crow Shivers as he came from the outhouse. He smiled acknowledging his presence but was very surprised he had come so early. Crow always enjoyed JT's company and considered him as one of his close friends. Climbing down from a top his horse as he extended his hand, he is met with a hearty hand shake and a slap on the arm as they turn and head for the front porch. Still barefooted Crow ascends the steps and sits in his chair as he follows. JT almost laughed out loud when he noticed how ugly Crow's feet were. Feeling plucky he made a comment about his feet that was simply answered by a sarcastic comment, "that's why I keep'em civered". They laugh together as JT hangs his hat on the back of the rocking chair just outside the front door causing it to rock slightly under its weight.

The noise of life in the background soon filled the air as the family mills about inside waiting for breakfast to be prepared. Suddenly the front door swings open crashing back against the side of the house as the oldest boy darts down the steps in a blur toward the outhouse letting the door slam shut. Immediately this action brought harsh reprisal from Crow. JT had never known this side of Crow and wondered if something had happened that morning to insight such an outburst. The boy stops in his tracks knowing he had committed an indefensible sin. The boy shamefacedly approached the steps cringing as he passed by his father. He cautiously opened the door and shut it again lightly, turned and said. "Sorry pa.

I gots ta pee." Turns and runs down the steps toward the outhouse. He could tell Crow did not like what had just happened but out of respect for his visitor he allowed it to pass without saying another word. By the time the boy made it to the outhouse one of his younger brothers had locked the door not allowing him to get in. Already annoyed Crow could not pay attention to what JT was saying for the ruckus raging at the outhouse. He dismissed himself and headed in that direction. JT was concerned because he had never known his friend to get this agitated or unfocused. Both boys received a whipping for their annoyance as Crow returned and asked where they were in their conversation.

JT nervously shifts in his seat very uncomfortable with the question he was about to ask, along with having to witness Crow's actions. The way he was acting caused Crow to become nervous as well. Crow hoped what he was trying to say was nothing bad until he told him about Sarah and his feelings. Crow sat back causing his rocker to squeak, very relieved it was nothing serious. A slight smile crossed his face as he begun to speak. His advice was to grab a good woman if you could find one he said, a matter of fact. He added he believed Sarah was a good woman and comes from a good family. Everything he said was encouraging him to marry her because he was not getting any younger or any prettier. He told him if it were he, he would plan the wedding for next winter. Then between now and he could take a last jaunt. He heard they were hiring surveyors up north and this would give him a chance to accumulate some money and marry her but not right now. The rest of the day was enjoyable as JT relaxed knowing he had finally come to a conclusion.

After saying his good-byes JT awkwardly walked toward Sarah becoming overwhelmed by her beauty on this particular morning. Her foolishness and forwardness he had witnessed that day on the creek was now absent. He hoped his decision to go away for a while was not the reason for her reserve but it was a chance he had to take. He gathered her into his arms without regard of who were standing near and kissed her assuring her he would be back very soon. He reluctantly climbs onto the back of his old horse, touches his side with his heels causing him to saddle up next to Sarah and tells her good-bye.

He rides west familiar with the landscape and very comfortable in this stretch of woods. He had always thought that this was the prettiest place he had ever seen and if the women he would marry loved these woods as much as he does then he would know she was the one. The instant he thought this he shook his head thinking just how silly he must sound using the love of this land as a gauge of his love for Sarah. He hoped no one would ever know how asinine he was. Crossing the big creek he then turns north. The first destination of this leg of his trip was Longwood to see Henry Tanner. While at the Magrit place they talked of him being ill and Crow feared he would not last much longer. JT had always respected the plain spoken gentleman and considered him as one of his greatest teachers. He was small in stature but a giant of a man in his compassion for other but firm in his dealings. Will respected this attribute in all men but found very few who posses it.

He lazily rode allowing his horse to set the pace. Aware of not having to be anywhere at any particular time he would just followed the natural opening in the scrub. While riding through a large cabbage hammock he happened across a small bunch of steers that looked to be about three years old. He was able to get a close enough look to see there was no sign of any mark on them. Thinking to his self it would be worth their time to come here next spring to see if they could rope them and put his mark in their ears. The wind switched and they winded JT as he rode close. They ran like deer through the thick growth. It always amazed him to see a slumbering cow as fleet footed as fleet footed deer.

It took a little over a day to finally arrived in front old white washed house. He had passed several large houses trying hard to avoid any contact with the strangely dressed northerners who asked too many questions. He liked being alone. As always he reiterated his vow that if the land around his place began to build up he would move to where there was no people. A sagging white wash picket fence stands in front of the house. Tying his horse out front, he beats the dust off his pants with his hands. He then removes his hat, rubbing his hand through his hair trying to straighten it. Stepping onto the porch and quietly knocks. Soon a little old lady comes shuffling from the back of the house, answering the door with a smile and a kind greeting. JT introduced himself when she told him she knew who he was and he was always welcome. He asked about Mr. Henry, she told him that he was not doing well. She continued by saying, "don't worry he may not recognize you." To which JT just shrugged his shoulders. She waddles into the room raising her voice calling out to Henry telling him young JT had come a long way to see him and he needed to wake up and be sociable. The old man roused slowly opening his eyes squinting through his small slit for eyes looking at JT with a wide smile. He reached out with his now withered hand. JT smiled and sat next to the bed waiting for the old man to speak but he was too weak to say anything. He began to tell him about Will Magrit's cows and the last time they gathered them. He described the bunch he saw while on his way to see him.

The old man relaxed, closed his eyes. JT thought he had fallen asleep but he only relived his life. His childhood, the first time he traveled into the wilderness of Florida, the first time he saw the big creek and his children. Life had been hard but good. His only regret was that he did not spend as much time teaching his children the most important things in life. Now that he was old, the only thing that really counts for anything is what you do for tomorrow. He was not referring to wealth this world, he was thinking about eternal things. It was the only solace he had in his last days was his faith. That if death was to come tomorrow he was ready hoping his children knew this as well. JT noticed he had fallen asleep and sat in silence until the old man motioned for him to continue. Before he could begin Henry's wife entered the room handing JT a steaming cup of coffee. He took a long sniff of the coffee relishing the memories that inundated his mind. She moved to the edge of the bed grunting as she tried to lift Henry to a sitting position. She strained until JT set down his cup of coffee and helped her. With a single movement he hoisted Henry up as she shifted the pillow behind him handing him a small tea cup. He could not believe how frail he had become. Sitting in silence he could see the steam rise as he labored lifting the coffee to his mouth.

JT sits in silence remembering the many stories he heard told around the many cow camps he had the privilege to be a part of. He watched the old man as he labored breathing and JT made up his mind he had traveled far enough. He knew right then he loved Sarah and was not willing to wait another minute. He wanted what Henry had knowing he did not want to live alone. Glass stood between him and several fancy hats on display. The man behind the counter laughed at his awkwardness and asked if he needed any help. JT stood then asked if he had anything that would make a good wedding present. "Who's getten married?" JT smiled and told him he was heading home and as quick as he gets there he was marrying the prettiest girl east of here. The man called to his wife who had moved closer so she could hear what they were talking about. She acted surprised when he asked her. She said with a strong Irish accent. "I have the exactly what you need" as she reached under the counter handing him a velvet box filled with fancy rings. He looked at her strangely. The expression on his face asked a million question. Her simple explanation was that all young men gave a ring to the women he was going to marry.

JT examined the rings and settled on a shiny one with a red stone. They called it a ruby. The ring was the prettiest thing he had ever seen and knew it was the one for Sarah. He paid the man four dollars then had it rapped. Putting in his pocket he stepped out onto the porch smiled and climbed into the saddle and headed south.

ABOUT THE AUTHOR

R. Wayne Tanner was born into a pioneer family having a long history reaching back as far as 1834, when his great – great grandfather came to Florida as a scout during the second Seminole Indian war. Wayne's family has ranched and farmed this area for generations. He is a loving husband and father. He has been married to Susan Henson Tanner for 24 years and has four children, Mrs. Susan Chesnutt, Jared Tanner 23, Sarah Tanner 20(R.I.P) and Hannah Tanner19. Being a 5th generation Florida Cracker Wayne enjoys sharing his love for farming and ranching with his family and friends. Wayne was called into the ministry and has been a Baptist minister for 23 years and is a bi-vocational pastor in the Kissimmee area.